Julie Beth Fasano?

The last time Hunter had seen her, she'd been a barefoot, gangly tomboy of eleven.

Looking at Len, his partner, Julie launched into a seductive rendition of "Happy Birthday."

This was no tomboy.

Their eyes met. The message seemed clear. She didn't recognize him, so he beckoned her closer.

To his surprise, not to mention Len's, she bent and gave the older man a quick kiss.

When she approached and gave him a questioning smile, Hunter blurted the first words that came to his mind. "My birthday's tomorrow."

Her dark-lashed eyes widened almost imperceptibly, and then, standing on tiptoe, she whispered, "Happy birthday," and touched her soft lips to his, immediately setting him on fire.

"Oops," he told her with a teasing grin. "Tomorrow's not my birthday."

She maneuvered past him. "I know." Shooting him a wink over her shoulder as she headed down the hall, she added, "Your birthday is in August."

Dear Reader,

There's no better escape than a fun, heartwarming love story from Silhouette Romance. So this August, be sure to treat yourself to all six books in our sexy, sizzling collection guaranteed to keep you glued to your beach chair.

Dive right into our fantasy-filled A TALE OF THE SEA adventure with Melissa McClone's *In Deep Waters* (SR#1608). In the second installment in the series about lost royal siblings from a magical kingdom, Kayla Waterton searches for a sunken ship, and discovers real treasure in the form of dark, seductive, modern-day pirate Captain Ben Mendoza.

Speaking of dark and seductive, Carol Grace's *Falling for the Sheik* (SR#1607) features the mesmerizing but demanding Sheik Rahman Harun, who is nursed back to health with TLC from his beautiful American nurse, Amanda Reston. Another royal has a heart-wrenching choice to make in *The Princess Has Amnesia!* (SR#1606) by award-winning author Patricia Thayer. She survived a jet crash in the mountains, but when the amnesia-stricken princess remembers her true social standing, will she—can she—forget her handsome rescuer...?

Myrna Mackenzie's *Bought by the Billionaire* (SR#1610) is a Pygmalian story starring Ethan Bennington, who has only three weeks to transform commoner Maggie Todd into a lady. While Cole Sullivan, the hunky, all-American hero in Wendy Warren's *The Oldest Virgin in Oakdale* (SR#1609), is coerced into teaching shy Eleanor Lippert how to seduce any man—himself included.

Then laugh a hundred laughs with Carolyn Greene's *First You Kiss 100 Men...* (SR#1611), a hilarious and highly sensual read about a journalist assigned to kiss 100 men. But there's only one man she *wants* to kiss....

Happy reading—and please keep in touch!

Mary-Theresa Hussey

Mary-Theresa Hussey
Senior Editor

Please address questions and book requests to:
Silhouette Reader Service
U.S.: 3010 Walden Ave., P.O. Box 1325, Buffalo, NY 14269
Canadian: P.O. Box 609, Fort Erie, Ont. L2A 5X3

First You Kiss 100 Men...

CAROLYN GREENE

SILHOUETTE *Romance*®

Published by Silhouette Books

America's Publisher of Contemporary Romance

This book is dedicated to Day Leclaire…
my friend, mentor and constant source of inspiration.

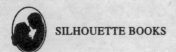

SILHOUETTE BOOKS

ISBN 0-373-19611-3

FIRST YOU KISS 100 MEN…

Books by Carolyn Greene

Silhouette Romance

An Eligible Bachelor #1503
Her Mistletoe Man #1556
First You Kiss 100 Men... #1611

Previously Published as Carolyn Monroe

Silhouette Romance

Kiss of Bliss #847
A Lovin' Spoonful #912
Help Wanted: Daddy #970

CAROLYN GREENE

has been married to a fire chief for more than twenty years. She laughingly introduces herself as the one who lights the fires and her husband as the one who puts them out. They are a true opposites-attract type of couple and, because of this, they and their two teenagers have learned a lot about the art of compromise.

Coming together...mentally, physically and spiritually. That's what romance is all about, and that's what Carolyn strives to portray in her highly entertaining novels. Says Carolyn, "I like to think that after someone has read one of my books, I've made her or his day a little brighter. You just can't put a price tag on that kind of job satisfaction."

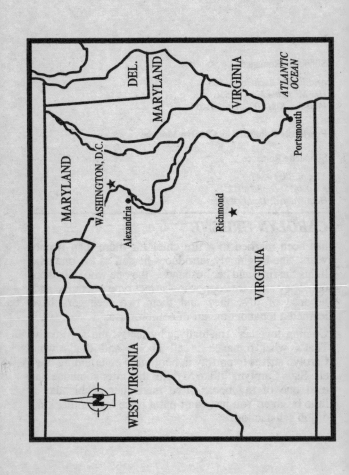

Prologue

Dear Ethel,
I'm seeing a man who's smart, funny and kind. How can I tell for certain if this is the right man for me?

Curious Carrie

Dear Carrie,
Unless some negative traits indicate he's not a good match, keep dating him. When the time is right, you won't need to ask anyone else's advice, you'll just know.

Ethel

"**Y**ou're making a wise move to fire Ethel and update this column," Julie said, hoping to win the editor's approval by validating his decision. A little sucking up during a job interview never hurt anyone. Especially when that someone's college degree was in theater costuming and she was applying for a journalist position with Virginia's prestigious *Richmond Reporter* newspaper. Hopefully, Mr. Upshaw wouldn't hold it against her that she'd changed career paths *after* graduation. "For example, this lame answer she gave—'you'll just know'—doesn't cut it. How can your Generation-X readers trust advice like that? They want answers that are black-and-white." She squinted at the small, grainy photo of the elderly columnist. "How old is she, anyway? I'd guess at least ninety."

The editor cracked his knuckles. "My aunt Ethel turned eighty-seven last month. And I'm not firing her. She's retiring."

Aunt Ethel? Julie swallowed. When would she learn to think before she opened her mouth? "I'm sorry, Mr. Upshaw. I have nothing against the advice of older people. In fact, my grandmother used to say stuff like 'a girl should kiss a hundred men before she marries,' so I got a journal and started keeping a list of all the guys I..."

The editor stared at her, saying nothing, so she impulsively filled the silence with the first thought that came to mind. "I could write about my grandmother's advice to see if it holds true in this millennium." She sat up straighter, excited about this fun new possibility. "It wouldn't be an advice column in the traditional manner of questions and answers, but you did say you wanted something different."

Her voice trailed off as she realized she was babbling from nervousness.

He rubbed his chin. "A column about kissing. That's different."

"There's lots of other advice I could research, too."

He seemed not to have heard her. "How would you find a hundred men to kiss?"

Writing solely about kissing was a turn she hadn't expected, but it sounded like an opportunity, and Julie wasn't about to pass it up. "Oh, I have a part-time job that introduces me to lots of men."

His eyebrows rose a notch.

"Not *that* kind of job," she added hastily.

Now he scratched his bald head, as if weighing the possibility of hiring her. Julie crossed her fingers in her lap.

"You suppose you've got enough material for a month of columns, three times a week?"

"Undoubtedly!" She wasn't so certain, however, whether her limited supply of kissable men would hold out for a month.

"I like your style," the older man said, rising to his feet.

Yes…! Julie followed him to the door, doing a little victory jig behind his back.

"We'll try you for a month, freelance and if you're any good you can stay on as columnist and take on some reporting duties as well." He blocked her exit with an arm across the open doorway. "But you'll have to remain anonymous during the trial period. Keep in mind that the ability to handle confidentiality is a major requirement for a reporter."

"Don't worry, I won't let you down."

Chapter One

In my limited experience, I've found that the most difficult part of kissing is the approach. Who makes the first move? Are the signals being read correctly? A kiss, especially the first one shared by a couple, involves a delicate dance of uncertainty...and anticipation.

Laughter pealed from the reception area, shaking Hunter's thoughts from the case he was investigating and making him wish, not for the first time today, that his secretary's month-long honeymoon was already over.

It was Monday, the first workday since his efficient assistant's wedding, and things were already going to Hades in a wicker basket. His much-coveted sense of order and calm was already being shattered.

Now someone was strumming what sounded like a ukulele, and a buzz of giggling and chattering voices sounded from the reception area. He had already rescued the company from near-collapse once. It wouldn't do to let things regress merely because Trudy and his top investigator had tied the knot. Better nip these shenanigans in the bud now and remind everyone to save their fun for the lunch hour.

Hunter closed the file and lined it up squarely with the right, near edge of his desk.

Out front, all the staff from Oltmeier-Matthews Investigation Agency surrounded his elderly business partner, Leonard Oltmeier. In addition, a number of employees from neighboring offices had come over to see what the noise was about, and had stayed to lend even more frivolity to the event.

Hunter stood in the doorway for a moment, hating to be the bad guy again. But if it hadn't been for his insistence on adhering to the strict policies and procedures he'd drawn up shortly after coming to work here, the company would have gone under a long time ago. Everyone who worked here appreciated the increased efficiency and higher salaries that resulted from following his rules, but old habits were hard to break. And most of the time Hunter was the one who had to remind them.

Like now. He sighed and stepped into the crowded reception room. His partner perched on the arm of the couch and smiled at a young, dark-haired woman who handed him an oversize greeting card. Hunter couldn't blame the old guy for abandoning work in favor of being serenaded by the lovely siren.

Of course! It was Len's birthday. Hunter cursed his rotten memory. If Trudy were here, she would have reminded him. But his secretary wasn't here, so he'd have to make do the best he could until her return. Meanwhile, he'd have to remind Priscilla, Len's secretary, to keep him posted on such matters.

Having handed the giant greeting card to Len, the brunette hit an off-key note on her ukulele, sang a few notes of "mi-mi-mi," and then launched into the "Happy Birthday" song. Her voice was untrained but enthusiastic...and somewhat familiar. Hunter moved into the room and positioned himself near the exit, hoping to get a better look at the woman in the Sherlock Holmes hat, but she was intent on giving the birthday boy her full attention.

The back view of her wasn't bad, though. Her slim-fitting pink body shirt, decorated with large black question marks, showcased the taper from ribs to waist, and a soft black leather skirt skimmed her narrow hips, falling to the middle of her thighs. Hunter drank in the view. By now, she'd switched to Marilyn Monroe's version of the song, going so far as to act it out by bending forward slightly and placing her palms on the tops of those mind-boggling legs.

The voice, though tickling his mind with its familiarity, left a lot to be desired, but that didn't matter as long as his gaze caressed her gently rounded rump. Hunter's body responded in a way that had him thinking of hot, sweaty nights and wrinkled sheets. He turned to leave before his libido led him to do something he might regret.

That's when the brunette turned, arms outstretched, and milked the final words of the song. "...to you...!"

Julie Beth Fasano? No, it couldn't be. The last time he'd seen his former neighbor, he'd been about to depart for college, and she'd been a barefoot, gangly kid of eleven. A tomboy who untiringly dogged his tracks, often inviting herself to accompany him on dates with her older sister.

He blinked and looked again. This was no tomboy. All traces of the scraggly hair, skinned knees and crooked teeth had evaporated, and in their place was a lovely young woman with below-the-shoulder curls, legs that seemed to go on forever, and sweet pouty lips that dared a man to kiss them.

Hunter took a couple of deep breaths as he assessed the changes that had taken place in his pesky former neighbor over the past dozen years or so. Half a lifetime for her.

She played to the audience, and their eyes met. Hunter gave her an embarrassed smile. The girl—er, woman—had always had a knack for getting under his skin. He just hoped she wouldn't know how much she'd affected him today. She returned his smile with a polite one of her own. Their gazes lingered a mere second longer, but it was enough time for him to notice the quizzical expression she shot him. The message seemed clear. She didn't recognize him.

It wouldn't hurt to stay and watch the rest of her performance. He wouldn't get any work done anyway as long as he knew she was still out here. Hunter joined the others as they applauded her overacted performance. To his surprise, not to mention Len's, she bent and gave the older man a quick kiss and once again wished him a happy birthday before gathering up her ukulele and car keys.

Lucky Len.

Lingering by the exit while Len's assistant tipped her for the singing telegram, Hunter moved to intercept Julie Beth on the way out. He would remind her who he was and watch her reaction. And maybe inquire after her grandmother.

But when she approached and gave him that same shy, questioning smile, the words in his head vanished. Neither spoke for a moment, and the silence hung awkwardly between them when he made no move to let her pass.

Her pale blue eyes darkened slightly. The fringe of dark, sultry lashes and the brash, upward jut of her chin reminded him she was no longer a child. Little Julie Beth wasn't so little anymore.

Seeing her standing there like that, her face tilted as if inviting him to partake in the kiss he'd coveted earlier, he blurted the first words that came to his mind. "My birthday's tomorrow."

Those dark lashes widened almost imperceptibly, alerting him that his remark had surprised her as much as himself. And then her freckle-spattered face was covered with a broad, uncensored smile. Standing on tiptoe, the ukulele dangling at her side, she whispered, "Happy birthday!" and touched her soft lips to his.

Forgetting about adhering to workplace procedures or saving social pursuits until the appointed break time, Hunter returned the kiss and felt himself respond in a way that was decidedly unprofessional. Not to mention painful.

It was as if she had locked up his brain and handed the key to his mutinous body. He pulled her to him, seeking release in the sweet sensation of her touch, but that only served to fan the flames even higher. And when she lifted her arms to encircle his neck, he didn't even care that she banged the ukulele against his rump.

Her mouth, which he remembered as being full of

sass and mischief, was now sweetly compliant as he explored her tender lips with his own. Her strawberry-flavored lipstick teased his senses, making him hunger for more. The soft curve of her breasts pressed against his chest, and Hunter damned the suit jacket he was wearing for adding an extra layer between them.

It was seconds—or maybe minutes, or even days—later when he reluctantly lifted his head to end the kiss. Julie Beth exhaled deeply and dragged her arms from around his neck. Her motions were slow, almost as if she were drugged.

"Hear, hear!" said Len in an appreciative tone. The rest of the staff signaled their agreement with cheers and thunderous applause.

Hunter swallowed. He didn't regret what he'd done, but he hoped Julie Beth wasn't embarrassed by the attention. His gaze still fixed on the delicate features of her face, he sought to lighten the mood and, at the same time, cut an escape hatch for himself.

He asked his partner, "What's today's date?"

"April first," the old guy said.

Julie Beth narrowed her eyes at him as she caught on to what was happening.

"April fool," he told her with a teasing grin. "Tomorrow's not my birthday."

She tucked the ukulele under her arm and maneuvered past him. "I know." Shooting him a wink over her shoulder as she headed down the hall toward the elevator, her skirt swaying in a devilish salute, she added, "Your birthday is in August."

"I think Anna is seeing someone."

If it were anyone other than his brother making this outrageous statement, Hunter would laugh and tell him to get a hobby and stop letting his imagination run amok. As a judge and a pillar of the community, however, Peter Matthews was not prone to creating fanciful tales.

"She's been slipping out at odd times of the day and night, and she refuses to tell me where she's going." Peter's face tightened in pain. He stabbed at the chicken with his fork. "And yesterday, when I looked in her tote bag for a pen, I found some racy lingerie."

Hunter's sister-in-law had been a devoted wife and mother during her eighteen years of marriage. As much as Hunter tried, he couldn't imagine her hurting Peter like this. Not intentionally, anyway. "There must be a reasonable explanation for her behavior."

"Things haven't been well between us for a while." Peter met his eyes and then looked away. "I want you to follow my wife. Find out what she's been up to. It's important that we keep this unpleasantness out of the media." He leaned forward and lowered his voice as if to emphasize the importance of what he was about to say. "With the reappointment coming up, I can't afford a messy scandal."

Hunter set his napkin on the table. He had no wish to get in the middle of their marital difficulties, but an impartial third party might be able to help them. "You don't need an investigator," he said gently, "but a good counselor could probably help."

Peter clenched his jaw. "I already suggested that to Anna. She wouldn't go."

"Did you offer to go with her?" He immediately answered his own question. "What am I thinking?

Of course not.'' Despite the fact that Hunter had always admired his high-achieving older brother, he recognized that Peter often had difficulty believing he could ever be less than one hundred percent right. Perhaps that's what had led him to become a civil court judge. It allowed him to have the final say on most of the cases that came through his courtroom.

Peter's high-handed attitude softened for a brief moment, long enough to make Hunter realize that his brother was deeply concerned. ''We have two teenage sons who need their mother.''

If Hunter hadn't already been swayed by Peter's worried expression, mention of the boys would have been enough to make him agree to take the case. ''After all you've taught me about collecting airtight evidence for my clients, I suppose I owe you a favor in return.''

The smile of relief that greeted his response was clearly heartfelt. Hunter didn't like what he was about to become involved in, but it would be worth the sacrifice if the results of his investigation provided a healing salve for his brother's marriage.

Hunter left the restaurant and walked the long way back to the office. He told himself it was because he needed the extra time to think about his brother's situation, but the decision had more to do with the fact that the Merry Messengers telegram shop lay along this route.

Curiosity was his motive, he told himself as he walked past the bagel shop and an independent bookstore. As he approached Merry Messengers, he slowed his pace and casually glanced in the window to see if Julie Beth might be there, waiting to deliver her next kiss-o-gram. As for what he would do if he should happen to see her, he hadn't thought that far ahead.

Holding a hand to his forehead to shade his eyes, he squinted into the dark store. A middle-aged woman behind the counter smiled and waved him in.

It wasn't Julie Beth. He took her invitation anyway, and once inside, glanced around the small shop.

Real and silk flowers adorned a shelf near the counter, and on the back wall sat ceramic figures and plaques with cute sayings. A spinner rack near a door marked Employees Only offered an assortment of greeting cards, a few of the less attractive ones gone yellow with age.

Still no sign of Julie Beth. He turned to leave, but the proprietress would have none of that.

"How may I help you today?" The woman spoke in an overly perky tone, as though she felt the need to demonstrate the enthusiasm with which their telegrams would be delivered. "We're having a special on birthday-grams this month."

"Uh, no, I don't think so. I was just looking for someone who was at my office earlier today." He glanced around for a sign of the miniskirted imp who'd kissed him this morning. "But Julie Beth's apparently out on a delivery."

The woman did a spaniel impersonation and cocked her head. "Julie Beth?"

"Julie Fasano. She's about so tall." He held his hand at shoulder level. Maybe the size of the shop was deceptive, and the lady had employed so many merry messengers that she couldn't keep track of them all. His guess was confirmed when someone came into the building from a back entrance and made a small commotion beyond the Employees Only door.

He continued his description. "Long dark hair, petite figure," he said, emphasizing the latter with a wavy motion of his hands, "and short leather skirt. Really great legs…and an even better kisser," he added with enthusiasm. "Oh, and she wears strawberry-flavored lipstick."

The woman's perky demeanor vanished. "You were the, er, birthday boy?"

"No, actually, I was just a bystander who happened to get lucky."

Her tone fairly bristled now. "I'm afraid I can't help you with your search."

"But you must know her." How could anyone meet Julie Beth and not recall her exuberant spirit and playful attitude? "She was the one who delivered a kiss-o-gram to the Oltmeier-Matthews Agency this morning. Perhaps you could check your receipts. It's bound to be in there."

"There's no need for that," she said, her voice curt and cold. "Merry Messengers is a respectable business. We don't deliver…*kiss-o-grams.*" If a person could sneer her words, that's exactly what she did. "And we don't encourage fraternizing between our employees and the clients. I'm afraid you'll have to find some other way to enlarge your social circle."

She stepped out from behind the counter as if to escort him to the door, but he moved to one side to gain an opportunity to set straight her misperception. "No, it wasn't like that at all. You see, it was only a birthday song and greeting card, followed by a little peck on the birthday boy's cheek…sort of a congratulations kiss."

The woman folded her arms across her chest. "I'm going to ask you to leave now."

He didn't need a two-by-four over his head to get the message. It had been a stupid idea to come by here and an even stupider idea to try to reconnect with his former neighbor. If he really wanted to find her, it would be a simple matter to look her up through other methods. After all, he was a private investigator.

But he convinced himself it was best they hadn't reconnected. As a kid following her wacky impulses, Julie Beth had driven him crazy. He consoled himself about the aborted search with a mental reminder that, despite the passage of years, she probably hadn't changed much in that regard.

Julie waited until the bell jangled over the main door to signal Hunter's departure before she eased into the front room. She hadn't intended to eavesdrop on their conversation, but the familiarity of the customer's strong masculine voice had captured her attention, and when he'd spoken her name, she'd been hooked. Julie couldn't help smiling as she remembered what he'd said about her legs.

The look on Mrs. Quarles's face melted the happy expression from her own. She was really in for it this time.

"First there's the ongoing matter of your attire," her supervisor said. She gestured toward the door Hunter had left through, indicating the matter he had brought to her attention. "And now *this*."

"I can explain...."

"Will it be as imaginative as your excuse for stopping traffic on Main Street by swinging like Tarzan from the stoplight to deliver a rush-hour proposal-gram?''

Julie thought she had made it clear why she'd donned the silly costume and stopped traffic for the occasion, but she explained once again. ''The client's girlfriend works at the zoo. It seemed the logical thing to do.''

''So you said. And then there was that incident of the adoption-gram on horseback on the courthouse lawn.''

''The little girl loves horses. The adoptive parents wanted to celebrate the event with something fun that the child would remember.'' Her supervisor wasn't any more impressed with her reasons today than she'd been shortly after they had occurred. Julie wrung her hands.

''You can still see hoofprints in the rose beds.''

''They say rose petals are very tasty, so you can't really blame the poor horse for wanting to sample them.''

''Those weren't the only unscripted performances you've given,'' Mrs. Quarles said, ''but kissing the clients will certainly be your last.''

''The way he told it sounds worse than it was,'' she began. Her boss seemed cynical, but Julie gave it her best shot. ''You see, I'm actually doing serious research on the subject of kissing, so I don't wind up with a dud of a dude. So I got this spiral notebook and numbered the lines from one to a hundred and drew columns for the date, the name of the kissee and where it took place.'' She paused. ''Do you want to see it?''

''Absolutely not.''

''Anyway, I've got something like forty-seven

names in my book now. Most of them—especially the ones I got while delivering my singing telegrams—were just little dry ones on the cheek. I don't really know how that would tell me anything about the guy, but I suppose they all count.''

''I've heard all I need to know about this.''

''But wait, I haven't finished. The scoring column is where it gets difficult. People with B.O. get the lowest rating...thank goodness I haven't run across that yet. The highest score is a 'Zinger.' Only one has come close to that.'' With an uncharacteristic display of prudence, she decided not to volunteer that Hunter had been the one to earn that particular honor.

''You may pack up your belongings, Miss Fasano. Merry Messengers won't be requiring your services any longer.''

Chapter Two

Then there's the matter of expediency. Sometimes one of the partners in a kissing couple is a bit more…hesitant, shall we say?…than the other. Hesitation does not necessarily signify reluctance, but it sure can add to the frustration level.

Back at Oltmeier-Matthews, the receptionist got up to lead her to Hunter Matthews's office.

"Please don't bother," said Julie. "I want to surprise him."

With the ukulele strap slung over one shoulder and her purse over the other, she headed down the right corridor past a glassed-in meeting room toward the man who had wrecked her carefully laid plans.

The secretary's desk outside his office sat vacant. Except for the fact that it was devoid of papers and folders, she might have assumed that the employee had stepped away momentarily. A deep voice floated to her from the inner office—a voice that only hours ago had set her heart aflutter, but now filled her with an urge to use her ukulele as a weapon over his head.

"Yeah, Pete, I told you I'd look into it. Don't worry, I'll make it a priority. But I still think you're making a mountain out of a molehill."

Taking the musical instrument in hand, Julie pushed the office door open, stepped inside and pointed the neck of the ukulele at him.

"You used to be like a big brother to me," she announced. Well, not really like a brother, but she wasn't about to admit that she'd once had a long-term teenybopper crush on him. "Is that any way to treat *family?*"

"Pete, I'll have to call you back." Hunter hung up the phone and rose from his chair. Then he untwisted the coiled cord and moved the phone an inch so that it was exactly catercorner to the edge of his desk. "Two singing telegrams in one day? What's the occasion this time?"

"I'm not delivering a telegram. In fact, thanks to you, that part of my life is now history." Standing across the room from him as she was, Julie thought it prudent to raise her voice so she could be heard. But given her frustration level at the moment, her raised voice quickly turned to something nearer a shriek. "What possessed you to go to my employer and tell her I was delivering kiss-o-grams and that you happened to 'get lucky'? You made it sound like I was hiring myself out to deliver more than just a song and a greeting."

If he was ashamed, he sure didn't show it. He should have been avoiding her gaze. He should have been bowing and scraping and apologizing profusely, but instead he stood there like a statue of some gorgeous Greek god and studied her face with unwavering attention.

"I'm sorry," he said, taking a step closer. "That's not what I intended to do."

She gave him a point for appearing sincere, but the road to you-know-where was paved with good intentions. An overly honest conscience raised the point that it was she who had deliberately bent the company rules of not fraternizing with customers. Hunter's role had merely been to bring it to her employer's attention. But that didn't stop her from venting her frustration over this setback in her career plans.

"Then what, may I ask, were you intending to accomplish by telling my boss I was doling out kisses indiscriminately?" She'd been very discriminating when she'd favored him with an early birthday kiss, but there was no way she could have made Mrs. Quarles understand that.

"I'm not really sure," he responded, in a much quieter tone than she'd been using. He seemed truly perplexed.

"You're not sure why you wanted to ruin my career? Or you're not sure why you set me up to look like a wanton woman?" It seemed as though her blood was boiling in her veins. Her face felt hot, her chest was tight and her vision became blurred as she tried to stare him down through the tears that had pooled in her eyes. Anger, she reminded herself. Stay focused on the anger, and don't think about how much it hurts to have your career opportunities slashed and burned by one reckless conversation. She took a deep breath to fortify herself for the final salvo. "You owe me big-time, Mr. Hunter Matthews. And I want you to pay up now."

She heard a rustling sound behind her, but was distracted when he stealthily approached her. Positioning his body close to hers, he reached toward her.

For the space of a millisecond, Julie thought that he might take her in his arms and kiss her again. And during that slow-motion fraction of time, she wanted him to do it.

Time had treated him well. Gone was the lean teen physique, and in its place was a body enhanced by firm muscles and a tailored suit. Further magnifying his physical appeal was the lithe confidence with which he moved—confidence gained from maturity and experience. It was an exhilarating combination, and Julie was not immune to it. He'd been a potent package before he'd left for college. Now he was absolutely stupendous....

Lifting her chin in anticipation, she took a breath to steady herself. Of their own accord, her eyelids lowered, and she ran her tongue over her parched lips.

His hand briefly touched her arm as he moved her slightly to one side, and her knees became like pudding. Then the contact was broken as he leaned past her to grab the door. Mmm, privacy.

"Sorry about the disturbance, folks. Everything's under control now."

Julie's lashes fluttered open. *Folks?* She turned just before he pushed the heavy wooden door shut and saw a half-dozen curious faces smiling at them. Most of them were the same people who'd watched as she sang to Mr. Oltmeier this morning.

With a barricade between them and their audience, they were alone again. But having been jolted out of her momentary distraction, and disappointed that the situation hadn't gone according to her secret wishes, Julie refocused her attention on the matter at hand.

"You owe me a job."

"That would never do."

"I don't think you understand how important the Merry Messengers job was to me. Losing that position is going to severely and negatively impact my career plans."

He had the nerve to laugh. "You delivered singing telegrams. What kind of stepping-stone is that? Were you hoping to someday deliver singing and dancing telegrams?"

Julie crossed her arms over her chest. "Of course not," she retorted. "I've already been a dancing banana."

Too late, she realized she had only provided him more fuel for his entertainment. Looking at it from his point of view, she supposed it did sound silly to tie her career plans to a ridiculous part-time job, but she couldn't tell him the real reason she needed the Merry Messengers gig. For one thing, it sounded disreputable to say it provided her with plenty of men to kiss. For another, claiming she needed kissable men to report about in her test column would betray the terms of the agreement she'd made with Mr. Upshaw.

"Just give me a job working here, and I'll let bygones be bygones." Maybe she should just drop the matter now and look for employment as a waitress, but this was a matter of principle. He *owed* her. Besides, it would be so cool to do the Dick Tracy thing.

As for the column, she'd have to find another way to meet potential kissers.

"I told you I can't do that."

"Why not? I saw a TV news magazine report about private investigators, and it showed how you spend days or even weeks following people around. Certainly a couple of extra eyes, ears and hands could help lighten your load."

Once again, he closed the distance between them. This time, though, he wasn't reaching for the door. He touched her chin with the crook of his finger, and Julie couldn't help wanting him to finish what she'd started in her mind a moment earlier.

Hope resurged in her heart as his finger trailed upward along her cheek. Brushing a tendril of hair away from her face, he stroked the curve of her ear. As he leaned toward her, his dark eyes heavy with passion, she felt as though her lungs were paralyzed by his heady nearness. Her body braced for what was to come, and the memory of the last kiss sent a warmth throughout her that pooled in the pit of her femininity.

He was so close she could feel his breath on her face. Her lips parted in readiness. And then it came. Apollo had landed. Unfortunately, it missed the mark and ended up on her cheek instead. A dry, brotherly kiss.

Disappointment flooded her soul and found release in the form of a heavy sigh.

"That's why we can't work in the same office." Hunter leaned back and tucked his hands in his pockets, a wry smile on his handsome features. "Something happened between us this morning...something

I'm not ready or willing to explore. I've accomplished too much here to risk it with an office fling.''

The cynic in her wondered if his reluctance for romance had anything to do with his former fiancée. No one knew why they'd broken up years ago; he was too much of a gentleman to talk about it. But that didn't stop people from speculating that Yvonne had been at fault. In fact, Hunter's silence on the matter may have contributed to that assumption. And they all hated her for breaking his heart.

All except Julie. Although she'd hated to see him hurting, she'd been secretly glad that he would not be marrying. Not that she could have taken advantage of his availability; she'd been in college at the time and certain that someone as handsome, successful and mature as Hunter would not be interested in anyone like her.

And now he'd made that perfectly clear. Julie straightened her spine. ''Don't flatter yourself. I have something to say about the matter, too.''

''Yes, and you've already said plenty.'' He picked up the ukulele she'd set on the chair earlier and handed it to her. ''I'd be happy to give you a good reference, though.''

''Your technique in discussing my work with employers leaves a lot to be desired.''

To his credit, he looked remorseful about his role in her dilemma.

''So are you going to hire me or what? I have bills to pay and…career goals to accomplish.''

Hunter paused, rubbing his thumb over the little scar beside his mouth.

Definitely a good sign. Julie grinned at his response.

"What? Why are you smiling? I haven't answered yet."

"Yes, you have. You always did that thing with your scar before you caved in and let me tag along on dates with you and my sister."

He conceded with a nod of his head. "I'll have to work on that." A moment passed before he added, "By the way, how's Charlene? I haven't seen her in ages."

Since their mutual breakup thirteen years ago, to be exact. Julie hadn't understood at the time why her sister had not been torn apart over their peaceable parting. Charlene had explained that their relationship had run its course, and she soon moved on to another boyfriend, but Julie had thought at the time that if she'd been in her sister's shoes, she would have been devastated.

"Charlene married Nathan Kleinschmidt. They just had their first baby, a girl, last month."

Becoming an aunt had been a momentous event for Julie. Not only did her tiny niece give her someone to dote on, but little Evie had also stirred a long-held desire for a child of her own. Seeing the baby watch her mother's face with an expression of pure love had triggered a need in Julie, a longstanding need that she'd only recently recognized. A need to be cherished.

Each time one of her former classmates had married, Julie had sat at the wedding, watching with envy the expressions of pure adoration the grooms had bestowed on their brides. Julie wanted to be looked at like that. She wanted to be the center of someone's universe. And the birth of her niece had opened a flood of feelings that had been growing for a long time.

"Please give them both my congratulations," Hunter said.

He studied her for a long moment, and Julie felt like she was nine years old again.

"As it happens, I am temporarily short on staff and could use you to fill in for about a month. I can't promise anything permanent, but it should keep you going until something else comes along."

Then he named a salary that was higher than her pay—even with tips—had been at Merry Messengers.

Working at a private investigation agency wouldn't give her much opportunity to meet new people, unless, of course, they happened to be lurking in a bush near hers. But it would keep food on the table, and maybe she could introduce herself to some of the people in the nearby offices.

"Deal," she said, holding out her hand to seal their arrangement. Julie did an admirable job of pretending not to notice the strength in his large hand, or the way his long fingers wrapped around her own. "You won't regret this."

"No offense," he countered, "but something tells me I will."

If he hadn't known better, he would have thought she was all set to attend a funeral...except no mourner would dare show up at such a solemn event looking as sexy as that.

The snug black turtleneck shirt would have shown off her trim figure, if not for the tailored, black leather jacket, which was zipped at the bottom. Then there was the skirt—also black and made of a touchable fabric—that slit enticingly over her left thigh. Sheer black hose and a pair of backless shoes finished off the ensemble. The only spot of color on her was the bright red lipstick that called attention to her wide smile.

Hunter fought to quell his physical response to the sight of her. Trying to focus on more professional matters, he led her to Trudy's desk. "This is your station. Active client files are in the bottom-right credenza drawer, the procedure manual is in the top right and stationery and supplies are on the left."

She looked perplexed. "This area is so open. How am I supposed to get any work done without some privacy?"

Now it was Hunter's turn to be puzzled. "This is the most effective arrangement. Since you're my right-hand staff, I'll need you to be accessible at all times."

Julie shrugged and tossed her black purse into the knee well under the desk. "I suppose it'll do. I'll be on the road most of the time, anyway, so it's not like I'll be shackled to it."

Hunter flexed his hand. If he were at his own desk, he'd be working the grip exerciser that he kept in the bottom drawer. It was a great stress reliever, and he had a feeling he'd be using it a lot during the next month. "On the road?"

She tilted her head, and a lock of soft brown hair fell forward over her shoulder. "Guess I'll have to study up on the lingo. Maybe you call it being 'in the field.'" When he failed to respond in the affirmative, she tried again. "'Research,' perhaps? Or 'on stakeout'?"

A groan escaped his throat. He hadn't spelled out that her duties involved only secretarial work, so she had filled in the blanks with a glamorized image of what she assumed her job would be. "Sorry, Julie Beth, but there will be no stakeouts for you." Remembering some of her childhood antics, he gave a little laugh. "Besides, I doubt that someone who used to be known as a Mexican jumping bean would be able to sit still during the long boring hours on stakeout."

"I'm not a child anymore." She crossed her arms at her waist, inadvertently drawing his attention to her flat stomach and the gentle curve of her hips. "I've grown up, in case you haven't noticed."

A man would have to be blind, deaf and paralyzed not to notice. Hunter took a moment to indulge in the awareness of those changes. For one thing, her voice had deepened from a childish soprano to a sultry alto. The youthful roundness had vanished from her freckled face, leaving delicately defined features that seemed at once expressive and mysterious. The changes in her body had been the most noticeable, but now that he considered her, he could see that even her attitude was different. She was still exuberant like the little girl who used to shadow his steps, but there seemed to be an underlying focus to her actions, as if she had somehow managed to harness her boundless energy and use it for a predetermined purpose. Such a potent combination could be either dynamic or disastrous.

She sat on the edge of her desk, the slit in her skirt parting in invitation, and kicked off her shoes in an ages-old habit that she had apparently been unable to conquer. To his annoyance, Hunter's thoughts led him to imagining her shedding other items of clothing. He flexed his hand again and chastised himself for his wayward thoughts. Julie was, after all, to be his secretary for the next month. It wouldn't do to start their time together by harboring after-hours thoughts.

Her gaze left his as she smiled at someone behind him. Hunter turned to see that one of his investigators, Ben Irving, had slowed his steps and seemed to be considering joining them. But a glare from Hunter helped him change his mind, and Ben continued on his way toward the file room, glancing over his shoulder at Julie. If Hunter's reaction was any indication, this was going to be a long, stress-filled month.

"I think I'd make a good P.I.," Julie persisted. "Just give me a chance, and you'll see."

A chance to do what? Wreck the cases he'd worked so hard to bring to fruition? Although Mark, one of his investigators, was honeymooning with Trudy, Hunter had no intention of turning Julie loose on Mark's cases. Those he would handle himself. "That's a very tempting suggestion," he lied, "but your duties will be primarily secretarial. My assistant is out on a month-long honeymoon, and I'll need you to keep things going smoothly until she returns."

Why did that last statement give him a funny feeling in the pit of his stomach?

"But I'm not cut out to be a secretary. I can handle detail work if it's for something I like doing, but typing and filing for someone else leaves me cold. I'm much more suited to surveillance work, and I'm good at it, too." Julie pointed a manicured finger at him. "I used to spy on you and Charlene all the time, and you never caught on."

Hunter couldn't help laughing. "I knew you were there. Your favorite hiding places were behind the sofa or the drapes. And sometimes you lurked inside the TV cabinet."

"You knew?" She seemed truly amazed, as if he were some kind of genius for having detected her whereabouts.

"Of course. You always took off your shoes, and your stinky feet gave you away."

Julie slid off the desk and slipped her shoes back on. "My feet didn't stink!"

To her chagrin, his only response was an amused chuckle, and then he launched into describing her job duties. *Secretarial* duties.

She interrupted his litany about filing procedures and telephone protocol. "Perhaps, as you said, my spying technique could have used some work, but I was only a kid then. With a little coaching, I'm sure I could do much better now."

"Forget it. Now, over here is the information on how to do Internet searches and—"

"Maybe I'll ask Mr. Oltmeier about letting me track down the bad guys." As a teen, Hunter had lorded his seniority over her, telling her what to do as if she had no choice in the matter. But she had quickly learned that going over his head to Gran or his mother had often garnered the results she wanted. Such as permission to accompany him and her sister to the ice-cream parlor for a sundae. "His name is first in Oltmeier-Matthews, you know."

There, let him deny that.

Without speaking a word, Hunter merely raised an

eyebrow. The gesture told her in no uncertain terms that such one-upmanship tactics wouldn't work here.

"All right, I'll do the stupid desk work. But I don't have to like it."

He flashed her a smug smile. "Good girl."

"But I have a few terms of my own."

If she didn't set firm limits right from the start, he might get the idea she was still a little kid that he could order around at will. And she wasn't about to let that happen. He tried the raised eyebrow thing again, but she didn't let it get to her this time.

"First, I don't want you talking to me like I'm still a child. I'm an adult now, with a college education, and I expect to be treated accordingly." She neglected to mention that her degree was in theater costuming. No need to undermine herself by offering too much information.

"Fair enough," he agreed.

"And don't call me Julie Beth. It's just Julie now."

"Done." He extended his hand and gripped her fingers in his warm grasp. Julie felt a tingle surge all the way to her toes. "Welcome to Oltmeier-Matthews."

He released her hand much too soon. She stood there feeling awkward, wishing she had pockets in which to thrust her hands, the right one of which seemed to still burn from Hunter's touch.

"Now I suggest you take some time to go through the files and familiarize yourself with the cases. The information in them and the way they're organized will give you a good idea of what we do around here."

"Files," she grumbled. "Spying would be more people-oriented."

Hunter picked up a few of the client folders from the open drawer and dropped them on her desk. "These *are* people. I suggest you treat them with care."

Julie released a disappointed sigh. How on earth, she wondered, would she ever meet any kissable men while stuck at this desk?

After transcribing the final sentence of the letter, Julie took off the headphones, typed in the signature lines and turned up the volume on the radio that crowded her desk. If she couldn't enjoy the work, she'd at least entertain herself by listening to the prank call of the day. She blew a bored sigh when Hunter brought her another cassette tape jammed with dictated letters, memos and instructions.

"Everything going okay?" he asked.

"Hunky-dory," Julie replied with more than a hint of sarcasm, and stuck a report on the stack of papers to go to Spencer in accounting. Truthfully, *mundane* was a more fitting description of how things were going. "You know, I really would do fine on stakeout. All this nitpicky paperwork is a waste of my talents."

Hunter reached over and transferred the report from Spencer's pile to Priscilla's. "If you can't keep a proper handle on this 'nitpicky paperwork,' how can you expect to handle a delicate matter like surveillance, which requires so much attention to detail?"

It would be different if the paperwork was relevant to something Julie liked doing. Like reporting. But spending all day shuffling papers for someone else's projects seemed pointless.

Hunter gave her a smug wink and returned to his office.

Julie bit her tongue to keep from hurling a scathing comment at his retreating form. Instead, she turned her fury on the keyboard, jabbing the keys as she punched in the command to print the letter she'd just typed.

"I'll show him," she vowed. If he wanted attention to details, then that was what she'd give him. Julie Beth Fasano would be so meticulous, so methodical and so, well, *mundane* that he would have no excuse for refusing to allow her on his surveillance outings. She would be so perfect, so particular and so persnickety that—

The printer jammed.

Unwilling to risk gobbing up the machine with paper, she went to the computer and hit a key to cancel the print job. The letter disappeared from the screen.

Julie stifled a scream of frustration.

"Is that letter to Mrs. Huffnagle ready yet?" Hunter called from his office.

"It's coming along." There was no telling *when*, but she'd get it to him eventually.

"Great. How about turning that radio down a bit."

The last wasn't a request, but an order. She lowered the volume and slid her shoes on in preparation to go look for Mr. Oltmeier's secretary, who might be able to help her unjam the printer and retrieve her lost document. Spencer chose that moment to pick up the papers she'd been intending to deliver to him. He gave her an assessing smile.

In return, Julie pushed a jar of toffees toward him. "How much candy would it take to persuade you to help me with this stupid computer?"

Spencer shook his head. "I don't have much of a sweet tooth. But there is something much more appetizing that you could bribe me with."

One corner of his mouth lifted in anticipation.

Julie automatically assessed the accountant's kissing potential. In the looks department, he was okay, despite the fact that he used a tad too much gel on his artfully styled, dark-blond hair. His face was handsome in a slightly better than average way, and his slate-blue suit gave an impression of good taste while carefully concealing the beginnings of a paunch. From what little she knew about him, Spencer seemed nice enough, but she wasn't interested in him as dating material. Even so, he'd probably stolen his share of kisses and might be willing to enlighten her with the benefit of his experience. And give her something to write about in her column.

She smiled and self-consciously straightened the turtleneck collar at her throat. "I suppose that's something we'll have to negotiate."

He graciously let the subject drop as he moved behind her desk and hunched beside her to maneuver the computer mouse. While he worked to retrieve the document, the radio deejay chattered on about how many calls he'd received that morning.

"I just don't understand all the commotion over a silly newspaper column," the deejay continued. "It seems like everyone in Richmond is asking who this mystery kisser is. And they're all calling us, as if we should know."

Julie felt her eyes nearly pop, then struggled to

maintain an attitude of nonchalance as the radio aired a conversation with one of the curious callers. Slipping her shoes off once again, she leaned back in her chair and worried how this might affect her chances for employment with the newspaper.

"What's the matter?" Spencer asked as he moused his way around the computer screen.

"Nothing," she said a bit too hastily. Glancing at him out of the corner of her eye, Julie saw that he didn't seem to notice her unease. Emboldened, she decided to probe for his reaction to her column. "I was just thinking about that mystery kisser they were talking about just now. I haven't read the paper yet— did you see the column?"

Spencer hit the enter key. "Oops."

Hunter chose that moment to emerge from his office and ask for the Lifeway Insurance file.

Spencer straightened and handed her the mouse. "Sorry I couldn't help you."

After he left, Julie stood up to block Hunter's view of the cryptic error message on her computer monitor. It was still her first day. The last thing she wanted was to let him know she'd managed to mess things up already.

He took the file she handed him and paused to stare down at her. "You weren't that short this morning."

Without moving from her position, Julie stretched a toe toward the black mules hiding under her desk. "I, uh..." She gave a little laugh. "My shoes temporarily went AWOL."

He glanced down at her nylon-clad feet, then ever so slowly pulled his gaze up her body until his eyes met hers. He grinned knowingly, and the suggestiveness in his smile made her wish it was August already so she could give him another birthday kiss. "Perhaps you should ask Mr. Oltmeier's secretary to help you retrieve Mrs. Huffnagle's letter."

Julie hurriedly slid her feet into the recaptured shoes and made a move to leave, but Hunter stopped her with a hand on her arm.

"Before you go, I'd better warn you that Priscilla is a notorious matchmaker. She has tried to fix up her bachelor brother with every single female in the office."

Julie smiled broadly. Another potential kisser.

Hunter appeared irked by her reaction. "Why are you looking so happy? I'm trying to warn you not to let her sic her brother on you." He shifted the folder to his other arm. "And while we're on the subject, you should probably stay away from Spencer, too. He's totally trustworthy where numbers are concerned, but that kind of integrity doesn't always follow him into his social life."

Once again, Julie felt like a ten-year-old being lectured by her older, more worldly brother. She clenched her teeth and accidentally bit her cheek. With a grimace, she sought to remind him once again that she wasn't the little girl next door who needed to be reminded not to run into the street.

"I'm stating the obvious here, but you're my boss, not my date filter."

His eyebrows pulled together in the frequently used expression of his youth. He had done that a lot when they were neighbors, mainly when Julie had used her own form of logic to explain whatever mischief she'd managed to get herself into.

"Huh?"

She paused for a second, reminding herself that Hunter wasn't normally the type to interfere in her personal life. The only times he'd ever butted into her business were when he was concerned that she might get hurt. Like the time he'd caught her trying to make an explosive out of cap-gun powder. So she sought to reassure him. "Thanks to you and Gran, I've accumulated all the savvy advice I'll ever need. You don't have to worry about me anymore."

"Yeah, but you still see only the best in people, sometimes even when they don't deserve it." His expression turned serious, as it had when they used to hold their philosophical discussions about whether cats had nine lives or lemmings really committed mass suicide. "I don't want you to get hurt."

She lifted her chin. When would he understand that she was no longer an impulsive child who needed his protection? "I can take care of myself. Contrary to your long-held opinion, I'm not an accident waiting to happen."

At that moment, the deejay announced his return from the commercial break with the sound effect of shattering glass. Julie started at the noise, and Hunter gave her one of those knowing looks that once again managed to make her feel as if he had read her very thoughts.

His response was a resigned sigh. "When you talk to Priscilla, ask her to block out some time every day for the next week to give you some intensive training."

He turned to head back to his office, pausing only long enough to straighten one of the stacks of papers on her desk.

Julie popped a toffee into her mouth and tossed the wrapper into the trash can. This next month was going to be a long, hard one.

Chapter Three

Everyone loves a good mystery. Some people like it in movies or books. Others, such as doctors and scientists, attempt to solve mysteries in their jobs every day. Me? I like a bit of mystery in the man I'm kissing.

The man on the phone sounded a lot like Hunter. But why would he be calling from his office while he was with a client?

"Hunter, is everything all right?"

He cleared his throat and tried again. "This is Peter Matthews, Hunter's brother. Is he in?"

It took Julie a moment to adjust to the fact that the voice on the phone didn't belong to her employer. A span of about nine or ten years separated the brothers in age, which meant that Peter had been practically an adult by the time she was born. Although he hadn't been around much as she was growing up, she had seen him occasionally during holidays and his frequent visits home. And at his father's funeral. Hunter had taken the elder Matthews's death very hard.

His father, a policeman, had been killed in an on-duty accident when his partner had failed to follow a standard safety procedure. For a brief time Hunter had followed in his dad's footsteps and worked in law enforcement before leaving it to work at the agency. Julie supposed the accident was also the reason Hunter had become such a stickler for policy and procedure.

"Peter, it's nice to talk to you again. This is Julie Fasano." A pause followed while he apparently searched his memory to place the name. "I used to live next door to you."

"Julie?" he asked, as if still unsure who he might be talking to.

"You might remember me as Julie Beth."

"Oh, yes, Julie Beth! The little girl who used to come over all the time and mooch cookies. So you're working for my brother now, eh?" He chuckled softly. "I'd love to be a fly on the wall for that."

"Well, actually, it's been fairly uneventful." Manners kept her from telling the full truth—that the job was *boring*. "Hunter is meeting with a client right now. Would you like me to get him for you?"

She supposed she shouldn't interrupt him, but this was his brother and it might be important. Besides, she was curious about the discussion between Hunter and his client, and if she had an excuse to go in there, she might catch a portion of their conversation. Better yet, she'd love to actively participate in finding the daughter that the elegant Mrs. Dexter had given up for adoption nearly forty years ago.

"No, but you can give him a message for me."

Rats! Julie frantically searched for something to write on. In the process, she knocked a cup of pens onto the floor. Picking one up, she uncapped it and started scribbling on the closest bit of paper available—the margin of the newspaper in which she'd been reading her column. Peter started talking, but the ink refused to flow.

"Hold on a sec." She dragged the tip across the paper a few times before a spot of blue emerged. "'Check to see if...' What was the rest?"

"If the subject we discussed recently might be the mystery kisser."

For a moment, it seemed as though Julie's heart forgot to beat. Surely he couldn't be referring to her column? And who was this "subject" he'd mentioned? "Did you say 'the mystery kisser'?"

"Yeah. It's the new column in the newspaper that everyone's talking about. Today's article gives me reason to believe she might be the author, 'Ann Onimus.'"

"Oh my." Julie wondered if it would be prudent to probe for a name.

"Yeah, that was my reaction, too."

Julie hesitated before asking her next question. It was important to find out more about this curious development, but she didn't want to let on that her interest was more personal than professional. "I'm afraid I don't understand the significance. Why would Hunter want to know who's writing a column about kissing styles?"

"He doesn't."

She allowed a moment of silence to follow Peter's statement, hoping he'd fill it with a more in-depth explanation. He didn't.

"Just give him my message," Peter continued. "He'll know what it's about."

"Sure. I'll do that." With any luck, Hunter might be a bit more forthcoming than his older brother had been. And someday pigs would fly. But she could certainly give it her best shot.

"Good luck in your new job."

With the way things were going lately, she was going to need more than luck. Whether Hunter liked it or not, she was going to have to do a bit of sleuthing of her own.

For the next quarter hour, Julie resisted interrupting Hunter's meeting. The conversation with Peter consumed her thoughts. She tried to distract herself from worrying about it by focusing on a case in which a Mr. Younce was claiming disability benefits for a work-related back injury. Hunter had already explained that much of their business involved investigating insurance claims that were suspected of being fraudulent. Lifeway, the insurance company with offices in the same building, provided them with a lot of these cases. As for Mr. Younce's supposed incapacitation, the man had reportedly been seen doing yard work and even demonstrating some wrestling moves to his young son. Although it would thrill Julie to catch the dishonest scumball in the act of scamming his employer, the mounds of paperwork attached to the Younce case left her cold.

Muttering under her breath, she chanted, "Bored, bored, bored, bored."

Julie moved aside some folders to turn up the radio. Though she doubted her column would still hold the public's attention after yesterday's brief discussion, she tuned in anyway. A popular rock tune was playing, and she noted that the *Burning Issues* talk segment was another twenty minutes away.

Too antsy to sit still for that long, she carried the newspaper to Hunter's office door and listened to hear if the meeting was almost finished. The heavy wood effectively blocked most of the sounds, so she stepped closer and pressed an ear to the dark oak. No luck. Just some general murmuring sounds that she couldn't distinguish.

With a flip of her hair, she pressed her ear more firmly to the barrier. In almost the same instant, the knob clicked, the door swung open and Hunter leaped forward to catch Julie as she fell inward toward the surprised pair.

"Goodness!" said Mrs. Dexter, staggering back a step.

Bracing herself with a hand on Hunter's firm abdomen, Julie regained her balance. Time slowed as she breathed in the clean, masculine scent of him, and she briefly forgot that he was the boss and she was the secretary. She even forgot there was another person in the room with them. All she was aware of while she clutched his waist was that he was a man and she was a woman. And she wanted to investigate him with every one of her senses.

The moment passed all too quickly, and reality returned to her with an unwelcome jolt.

"I'm sorry for startling you both," she said, recovering her composure. "I was checking to see if your meeting was almost over."

Hunter flexed and relaxed his left hand, causing

Julie to wonder if he was itching to wrap his fingers around her neck. But then she remembered his habit of counting to ten during those times when she'd tested his patience during her childhood. Perhaps the hand-flexing was a grown-up substitute.

"I trust you found what you were listening for," he said. It was clear by the dryness in his tone that he suspected she'd been listening for more than just the conclusion of their meeting.

Of course she hadn't! But not for a lack of wanting.

"I have a message from your brother," she said, handing him the newspaper. "It sounds important."

Hunter obviously didn't buy her story, but didn't call her on it in front of his client. Instead, he thanked her for the message, said his goodbyes to Mrs. Dexter and retreated into his office.

Julie smiled at the tiny lady and led the way to the hall, where she pointed her to the reception area and elevator. Mrs. Dexter started down the hall, then halted and turned back toward her. "They say Mr. Matthews is good at what he does."

"You wouldn't believe what a perfectionist he is." That was definitely the understatement of the year. "If there's any way that your daughter can be located, Mr. Matthews will find her."

Mrs. Dexter nodded. "He has a reputation for being the best at what he does, which is why he can charge those high fees."

From the look of her expensive suit and stylish shoes, it appeared that Hunter's fees were of small concern to her. But Julie felt compelled to reassure her. "I'm sure you'll get your money's worth from his search."

"I have no doubt about that. But I do think you should ask him for a raise." She grinned and pointed her leather purse at Julie's stockinged feet. "He ought to be paying you enough to buy some shoes."

Julie glanced down at where her toes wiggled in the thick carpet. So accustomed to going without shoes, she had forgotten to slip them back on when the client had arrived. She would have been apologetic about her forgetfulness, but Mrs. Dexter spared her the explanation when she retreated down the long hall.

On the way back to Hunter's office, Julie paused long enough to step into her shoes, then went inside and flopped comfortably in his guest chair.

He looked up from the newspaper. "Is there a problem?"

"That's what I was going to ask you. Do you need any help reading my message?" Truthfully, she'd rather he read her lips.

"This one's pretty straightforward," he said, tossing the paper onto his immaculate desk. Julie wondered how he ever got any work done in such a neat environment.

"Thanks. I'm doing my best."

She couldn't blame him for not appearing comforted by her statement. From what she'd heard about Hunter's ever-efficient secretary, Julie's best day couldn't even measure up to Trudy's worst. She sighed, wishing once again that her boss would let her do some fun stuff. Like dressing up in disguises and following the bad guys into seedy bars. Then she'd cozy up to them, talk in a husky Kathleen Turner voice and get them to spill their guts by—

"Is there something else?"

Julie shook herself out of her reverie. "Yes," she said, forgetting to couch her question in subtlety. "Why does Peter think this person you two talked about is the mystery kisser?"

Hunter studied her for a long moment, and that was when Julie remembered she should have used more discretion. Unfortunately, the roundabout approach was not her specialty, which might be a disadvantage when he eventually let her tag along on his spy missions. And it was only a matter of time before she would wear him down. After all, she'd had plenty of practice getting under his skin. With so much experience, she knew exactly which of his buttons she needed to push to get what she wanted from him.

"I don't know," he said, "but I intend to find out."

Hunter picked up the paper again and read the message Julie had scratched onto it. Why hadn't she just used one of those pink message pads for writing the note? She probably couldn't find one for all the clutter on her desk. He reached into the bottom desk drawer and pulled out the grip exerciser. This thing had been getting a workout ever since Julie's arrival yesterday.

As he squeezed the spring-bound handles, his gaze fell to the front page of the *Flair* section. Below her scrawled handwriting, an image of a pair of red lips drew his attention to a column called "Uncommon Wisdom." The headline on today's piece was A Bit of Mystery. Curious, Hunter read the opening paragraphs and discovered that this was the work of the mystery kisser—the same person his brother had mentioned. He checked the byline. Ann Onimus.

Anonymous.

Glancing through the rest of the column, he wondered why anyone would want to read, much less write, this stuff. Who cared whether people kissed with their eyes open or closed? What did it matter if there was a sense of mystery in a kiss as long as the couple cared for each other? Apparently, this column was causing quite a stir in the community, but he just didn't get the appeal. Then again, he didn't get techno music, either, so who was he to judge?

Setting aside his personal prejudices, he read a portion of the column again, this time with an eye for clues that would have made his brother suspect Anna of writing it. Clues that tied her more closely with the column than the mere fact that she had taken a couple of creative writing courses in college.

The closed-eyes approach is always good for maintaining an air of enigma. That way, the physical imperfections can be ignored, though I must confess to a particular preference for an intriguing scar that hints at a rough and dangerous past.

As I set out to find a kissable man, I am careful to keep my identity as the mystery kisser a secret. When today's "kissee" came through with the goods, I couldn't help but wonder at the thrill that accompanied the mere touch of lips on lips. Ultimately, I chalked it up to the mystery enshrouding our coming together.

But it's also possible that the very mystery surrounding my identity and the fear of discovery add a heightened awareness to the game, for although people may enjoy reading my exploits, such antics would be frowned upon by men of husband material.

Okay, so what about this revelation had led Peter to think Anna was the writer? His brother had indicated that his wife had been acting restless and dissatisfied lately, but that was probably understandable after eighteen years of marriage. If most midlife crises hit women in their forties, then Anna was approaching that time frame. Perhaps she was seeking the spice and adventure she wasn't getting at home.

The clincher, however, was the last sentence. "Such antics would be frowned upon by men of husband material." Especially if that husband material was also judge material who had a professional reputation to protect.

And then there was that corny byline, Ann Onimus. If Anna was trying to conceal her identity, would she choose a first name so close to her own?

Personally, Hunter suspected it could have been written by any of thousands of women in the city. He felt fairly certain that it was a Richmond writer, given the references to local landmarks. Sure, there were numerous other hints throughout the article that the author could have been his sister-in-law, but they were all so vague it would be impossible to pinpoint one person as the culprit.

Folding the newspaper into a neat rectangle, he carried it out to Julie's work station. Perched nonchalantly on the near corner of the desk was a representative from the Lifeway Insurance Group on the eighth floor, a man who seemed to be enjoying himself too much for Hunter's peace of mind. His temporary secretary must be some kind of man magnet. Not counting Len Oltmeier and the elderly maintenance man, the Lifeway guy had to be the fifth or sixth man drawn to Julie's desk this morning. And it still wasn't even ten o'clock yet.

Hunter stood close enough to brush shoulders with him. "Is there something I can help you with?"

As he had hoped, the gesture was taken as one of intimidation, and Lifeway Larry immediately retreated from the desk to stand with military rigidity in front of them.

"Oh, no, sir. I was just bringing some extra information about the back-injury case." He smiled at Julie and reached over to pat the file that sat beside a box of doughnuts. "It's all right here, ready to be researched."

"That'll have to wait. Right now I need Miss Fasano's assistance on a more pressing matter."

She looked hopeful. Did she *really* think he was foolish enough to let her help tail a suspect? Judging by the way she hurriedly got rid of Larry, she apparently did.

"I'll take that folder," Hunter said, indicating the one that had just been added to her In box. "I'm going to spend most of the day watching for this guy to mow his lawn, and I'll need your help with—"

"Hold on while I find my shoes." Her eagerness revealed that she had already finished his request in her mind—with her own preferred spin, of course.

"—*researching* at the newspaper office."

Obviously crestfallen, she froze in the midst of her search. Scooted way down in her chair like that, with her toes stretched to make contact with the wayward shoes, she looked like a child in a chair that was too big for her.

No, strike that; she did *not* look like a child. There were too many bumps and curves to remind him that little Julie Beth was a woman now. A woman whose exuberance captured the attention and affection of everyone she happened to meet. In the brief time she'd been working here, she had already managed to meet almost everyone in the building. The women thought she was adorable and were arranging to introduce her to their brothers and single friends. And the men were making nuisances of themselves, inventing trumped-up excuses to loiter at her desk. The trouble was, Hunter wanted the same thing they did—a chance to spend time with the girl who used to pester him but now intrigued him. And perhaps the opportunity to steal a kiss or—

Snap out of it, Matthews! If he couldn't control himself any better than this, then it was a good thing he was leaving the office—and temptation—behind for the day. Ordinarily, he didn't go out on surveillance unless they needed additional manpower. With Len about to retire, Hunter had taken on more of the management responsibilities and thus spent much of his time in the office. But considering the recent developments, and the fact that his best investigator was honeymooning with Trudy, he decided he needed a break from the stresses here. Most notably Julie. Which was why he wasn't taking her with him on assignment as she hoped.

"The *Richmond Reporter* building is on my way to Younce's house. I'll drop you off so you can get copies of the past six months' worth of 'Uncommon Wisdom' columns."

"It's a new column," she blurted. "It's only been around since..." Her eyes widened as if she suddenly realized she'd spoken out of turn. "...uh, the last week or so."

"Okay, so bring me copies of *all* the columns."

She straightened in her chair. "Do you think that's really necessary?"

Hunter shrugged. "You could call and ask them to fax the columns, but it'll be quicker if you go and get them in person."

She didn't seem happy with that, but she reluctantly slid her shoes on and retrieved her purse. Hunter gave her a guarded once-over, taking in not only the sensuous sway of her body as she slung the trendy leather bag over her shoulder, but also the youthful post-college style of her hair and clothes.

He'd read only one of the mystery kisser's columns, but that was enough to clue him in that women like Julie were its target audience. Young, urban—and even urbane—professional women. Perhaps she could tell him why a little column about kissing could create such a big stir.

After they stopped to tell the receptionist where they were going, he pushed the elevator button. On the ride down to the garage, he asked for Julie's opinion on the matter.

"It's not as if it's earthshaking news," he protested. "So why does every woman under eighty suddenly feel compelled to read about someone else's kissing experiences?"

Julie tilted her head as if she, too, was baffled by the column's unusual success. "I'm not really sure. At first I thought it was because Richmond is a relatively small city, and women here were more receptive than they would be in New York or, say, D.C." She stepped through the door he held for her and followed him toward his sport utility vehicle. "But I think bigger-city readers might be interested as well. After all, kissing is a universal pastime."

He pointed the key tag at his car to unlock it, then went to the passenger side and held the door for Julie. "So is sleeping, but you don't see people writing about it in the newspaper."

She sighed as she slid into the seat, then waited until he joined her on the driver's side. "Maybe it has something to do with getting past the facade—the protective barrier that people put up around themselves. This is a hurry-up world, and people don't have the luxury of time for courting anymore. They want to be able to tell quickly and accurately whether their date is a potential lover or a loser. A prince or a frog."

"And a person's supposed to be able to tell all that from simple mouth-to-mouth contact?" He jammed the key into the ignition. "If you ask me, a kiss is just a kiss. No hidden messages."

He hoped she wouldn't go reading anything into that birthday kiss they'd shared. In fact, he didn't want to analyze it too closely himself, for fear there might be a hidden message lurking behind it.

"Oh, but it tells a lot about a person. Reading about another person's experiences and observations helps take some of the confusion out of the process. And perhaps it encourages them to know they aren't the only ones struggling to find the right man. They might even be secretly cheering on the columnist, as if by seeing her succeed at finding true love they'll know they have a chance at the real thing, too."

"You make it sound almost poetic," he said, firing up the engine. "I still don't understand all the mystery about something as simple as kissing. You either like a person or you don't."

He couldn't bring himself to look directly at her as he said those last words. In this case, it wouldn't accomplish anything to examine his own feelings on the subject too deeply.

Julie leaned back against the leather upholstery and hugged the purse to her waist. "Sometimes it's more complicated than that."

Hunter grunted and switched on the radio as he pulled out onto the street. "It must be a woman thing."

She shot forward and turned up the volume. "Shh! This is the *Burning Issues* segment."

When he flashed her a sharp glance, Julie immediately realized her mistake in showing too much interest in the subject. In an attempt to downplay her eagerness to hear the show, she offered a lame explanation. "These talk show hosts are really funny." Then she chattered on about previous *Burning Issues* and the hilarity that often accompanied the call-in discussions.

Hunter stopped for a red light and studied her for a long moment. Long enough for Julie to feel uneasy under his scrutiny. He used to aim those long, steady gazes at her when she was a kid, getting on his nerves. And she had learned early not to press her luck when he was in one of those moods.

But this time there was something different about the way he looked at her. The annoyance he used to show was missing, but he still seemed somehow bothered by her. Though she used to pride herself on

her ability to get under his skin, Julie had no idea
how she'd managed to do so this time. She only
knew that the heat of his gaze warmed her more than
all the kisses that she'd collected so far. Minus
Hunter's, of course.

Now that his name was on her kiss list, all the
other ratings paled in comparison. And, as pleasant
as Larry from Lifeway was, and as cute as Priscilla's
brother appeared in the wallet photo, their appeal
faded when measured against the man who now
drove her to the newspaper office—and drove her
crazy in the process.

A radio caller interrupted her thoughts as Hunter
pulled onto Regalia Avenue. "What I'd like to
know," the male voice said, "is what's the big deal
about kissing?"

Hunter smirked, apparently pleased at having been
validated by one of his own. His triumphant glance
at Julie served to enhance the clean, well-defined
lines of his face. The strong chin that carried an ever-
present hint of shadow, the angular nose that flared
gently at the nostrils and the dark eyebrows that
hooded equally dark eyes.

The radio caller continued, his voice deepening to
a note of false machismo. "You tell Ann that if she
wants to find out how a *real* man kisses, she oughta
come to Bubba. I'll give her a kiss that'll scorch the
paper that column is printed on."

"No can do," said one of the deejays. "No one
knows who she is."

"Bummer," the caller said.

They cut to a commercial as Hunter pulled the car
into a parking spot. "Who are you investigating?"
she asked, making no move to open the door. "And

why does your brother think she's writing a newspaper column?''

Hunter switched off the ignition and chewed at the corner of his mouth. ''Anna, my sister-in-law. Pete's wife.'' He briefly summarized how Anna had been spending many evenings away from home, detailed some of the similarities mentioned in the column and explained how his brother had come to the conclusion that Ann and Anna must be the same person.

''Do you think Anna is the mystery kisser?'' Julie asked.

Hunter relaxed back into his seat and let out his breath in a little whoosh. Apparently this had been occupying his thoughts a lot since he'd received his brother's message. ''I don't think so. At least, I don't *want* to think so. Anna has always been a devoted wife, so her secretiveness is very much out of character.'' Hunter loosened the knot in his necktie. ''My main concern is that she's not in any kind of trouble.''

Noting Hunter's concern, Julie bit her lip. She wanted to put his mind at rest and tell him that his sister-in-law was not sampling kisses with men other than her husband. But if she did, how would she convince him without explaining the truth about herself?

Her editor, Mr. Upshaw, had mentioned more than once that she should keep a low profile while working on her test columns. If Julie caved in and blurted her secret after only a week, how could he trust her with future assignments? And how could she expect to be considered for a full-time reporting job if she couldn't even handle a basic issue like confidentiality?

By nature, Julie was completely open and guile-less. Holding back like this went against her normal tendencies, which made her predicament even more difficult. But she had no choice. Not if she wanted to win the job with the paper. She decided it would help to look at the need for secrecy as practice for when she might eventually do an undercover story.

So, since she couldn't reassure Hunter with the truth, she offered the next best thing. "Want me to look into the situation about Anna and rule her out as the mystery kisser while you work on the Younce case?"

He gave her a long-suffering expression. "I don't need your help with investigative work. I need your help with the filing."

Julie pressed her lips together and made a rasp-berry.

The deejay returned from the commercial break and announced a new contest for listeners. A week-end trip for two to Atlanta to attend a twelve-hour "rock fest," was the prize. The task? Be the first to disclose the mystery kisser's true identity.

Julie froze, her hand on the car door's lever. She couldn't go into the newspaper office now. All of Richmond would be watching this building, taking note of who came and went through the large glass double doors.

"Is something the matter?"

"Uh, I was thinking about all that filing I have to do at the office. Perhaps it would be more efficient to have the newspaper fax me those columns."

Hunter looked skeptical, and rightfully so, given her previous resistance to doing routine paperwork.

"No," he said, handing her some cash to pay for

the newspapers and a cab ride back to the office. "I'm going to need those columns now more than ever."

She tucked the money in her purse and fixed her gaze on the man who had managed to recruit her in his efforts to ruin her own well-laid plans.

In explanation, he added, "Thanks to that contest, now I'm going to have to put a priority on Anna's case. If I can find out what she's been up to before the public gets wind of her activities, that may give Pete an opportunity for some damage control. And if it's not Anna, going public with the real kisser's identity would remove her from the list of possibilities. Besides, solving the case would give the agency some free advertising."

Still motionless, like a condemned woman awaiting the fall of the executioner's ax, Julie sat in stunned silence.

"What are you waiting for? We have a mystery kisser to catch."

Chapter Four

The search is on. The problem is that finding a
compatible kisser—and thus a compatible
mate—is not as easy as one might think. Personally, I like a man who's powerful, yet gentle. Thoughtful, yet daring. Generous, yet gets
what he wants. It isn't always easy to see at a
glance which traits a potential kisser possesses.
That's when you need to do a bit of detective
work and start putting two and two together.

"It's not fair that he stuck me at this computer,
searching for stupid bits of irrelevant data for three
whole days while he's out there having fun spying
on people. And speaking of people—" Julie waved
her mouse at Priscilla "—how am I supposed to
meet anyone with my leg shackled to this desk? I'm
going to die an old maid, I tell you!"

Priscilla pushed aside the procedure manual they'd

been going over, and gave her an indulgent smile. "You're young. There's plenty of time."

If only she knew. The newspaper columns Julie provided during the next three weeks would determine her fate as a professional journalist. And the success of those columns depended on the kisses she managed to score. She sighed heavily and kicked off her shoes. "I guess you could say my clock is ticking."

"Oh, hon, now you're being melodramatic." Priscilla handed her the back-injury file. "Tell you what, if you want to meet a nice guy to settle down with, let me fix you up with my brother. He's smart and sweet and handsome—you've seen his picture. You two would make beautiful babies." She studied Julie intently, as if imagining the progeny who would someday call her Aunt Priscilla. "What do you say? Let me fix you up while he's between girlfriends."

Under other circumstances, Julie would have said yes in an instant. However, the image that kept popping into her mind was not of the man in Priscilla's photo, but of Hunter's lean features and chiseled good looks.

First, he had ruined her opportunity to meet men through her Merry Messengers job. It annoyed Julie that now he was interfering with her opportunity to date a perfectly kissable man. Maybe she'd go out with Priscilla's brother later. But right now, the only man she wanted to kiss was Hunter.

"Thanks, Pris, but I'll have to take a rain check. Hunter's going to start putting me on surveillance duty soon, and I'll have to see what my schedule is like then."

Priscilla gave her a that'll-be-the-day expression, but said nothing.

"By the way, who's he scoping out this afternoon?"

Len's secretary pointed at the folder she'd just passed Julie. "He's at Gunther Younce's house, trying to get a video that'll prove the man is faking his so-called back injury. Then, later, Hunter said he'll be following someone he thinks is the mystery kisser." Priscilla twined a strand of strawberry-blond hair around her finger. "That one ought to be a lot of fun."

Julie felt her eyes widen. Picking up the Younce folder, she pointed it at her new friend. "For the past three days, he's had me confirming addresses and getting routine police reports. This is busy work, isn't it? He didn't need me to do this."

Priscilla shrugged. "It's stuff you would've had to learn anyway, someday."

The other woman's response confirmed what Julie already knew. "He was trying to keep me so occupied with paperwork that I wouldn't have time to think about going on surveillance. Well, I could be a good spy because I have something he doesn't," she told Priscilla. Tapping her chest, she added, "I have woman's intuition."

With that, Julie flipped open the file of the man Hunter was pursuing and scanned the contents, then summarized the police report aloud. "Looky here. This guy gets into a lot of bar fights, and he's a deadbeat dad for four different women. Do you think Hunter knows how to use this information to his advantage?"

Heedless of her new friend's lack of response, Julie slipped her shoes back on and slung her tiny purse over her shoulder.

"No...!" she continued. "Because if he did, he would have taken me with him."

Priscilla stood and positioned herself between Julie and the door. "Look, I don't think you should—"

Julie sidestepped her co-worker. "Would you be a dear and assign the necessary paperwork to someone else? I may be gone for quite a while."

"When Hunter finds out you broke protocol, you'll be gone for good."

Warm April sunshine beat down on the SUV, threatening to roast its lone occupant. Sweat beaded on Hunter's forehead, and he craved a cold soda. Two blocks behind him, a convenience mart sold fountain drinks over crushed ice, but he dared not move from his spot on Talazar Drive. He'd been here all afternoon, waiting for the shyster to come out of the house and prove himself to be the fraud Hunter knew he was.

The mail had been delivered ten minutes ago. Maybe that would entice the weasel out into the open. He wouldn't want to miss his "disability" check.

Meanwhile, Hunter adjusted the small video camera on the dash mount and sat back to wait. After he was finished here, he'd go over to the West End to see what his sister-in-law was up to. He folded back the paper and glanced again at the mystery kisser's column. Had her comment about doing "a bit of detective work" been a clue that Anna was on to him? He would have to take extra precautions to make sure he was not seen following her tonight.

The door at 418 Talazar opened, and a burly guy in a sleeveless T-shirt stepped out.

A movement at the passenger side of Hunter's SUV startled him out of his revelry.

"What's up? You stalking that Younce guy?"

His pulse racing, Hunter attempted to simultaneously focus the camera and wave Julie away from the car. To his chagrin, she didn't get the message. "If you're going to work for me, at least get the lingo right. I'm not 'stalking' anyone. Now get out of here before he sees us. People on stakeout are supposed to remain invisible to the subject."

She leaned closer and lowered her voice. "Don't be such a fuddy-duddy. You're never going to catch him by being invisible. Sometimes you have to put two and two together to figure out a guy's vulnerability."

Hunter shot her a fierce look but was distracted by the gap in her shirt, revealing a hint of cleavage. He licked his dry lips.

By now, Younce had retrieved his mail from the box by the road and was heading back to his porch. To Hunter's relief, the subject appeared not to notice the woman who seemed determined to blow Hunter's cover.

She stepped away from the car, lifted the hem of her top slightly and rolled the waistband of her skirt twice. This action shortened her skirt from mini to micro. Hunter swallowed hard. The temperature in the car seemed to climb by twenty degrees.

"Don't just sit there," she hissed in Hunter's direction. "Roll 'em!"

With that, she headed straight for Younce, her round little bottom swaying like a clock pendulum as she balanced precariously on ridiculously high heels. Invisible she was not. Hunter grimaced, wanting to stop her, yet was frozen helpless as his gaze fixed on the movement of her feminine curves.

With a bright smile, she approached the suspect and said something Hunter couldn't quite make out. Careful to make as little movement as possible, he positioned the video camera so that it captured the pair on film.

To his astonishment, Julie pointed in his direction. Hunter slid down in the seat. But he needn't have worried. Considering Younce's interest in her legs, it was doubtful the man would have noticed a purple cow.

Younce shook his head and pointed in the opposite direction, making a sweeping movement with his arm. Hunter chuckled despite himself. She was pretending to be lost, and asking the guy to help her find an address. Hunter didn't know whether it was intentional or just dumb luck, though he suspected the latter, but she had just provided him with proof that their shyster had full movement in his neck and shoulders.

Hunter's gaze went back to Julie. To her credit, she positioned herself so that Younce's mug would show clearly on the videotape. Hunter checked the focus as she took a step back and began digging through her purse. As she pulled out a scrap of paper, her keys fell to the sidewalk. Laughing, she bent as if to retrieve the ring of keys.

"No!" Hunter muttered under his breath. "Let *him* pick them up."

As if she had heard his thoughts, Julie stopped in midbend and coyly touched a hand to the hem of her barely there skirt. Hunter's body responded accordingly.

He held his breath. *C'mon, be a gentleman, you jerk.*

It was evident by Younce's hesitation that he'd rather watch her pick up the keys. Fortunately, chivalry won out, and the goggle-eyed man swept them up in a fluid movement that was both quick and graceful. Apparently smitten by the woman, he smiled and, placing one arm over his belly and the other at his back, gave her a courtly bow before handing her the keys.

Showing all of her charm and most of her teeth, Julie said something to him and then sashayed off in the direction he had pointed earlier. Younce craned his neck to watch as she rounded the corner, then heaved a large sigh and went back into his house.

Hunter waited a full two minutes before starting up his car and driving around the corner where Julie had gone. He found her sitting on a low wall, legs crossed, and one shoeless foot swinging impatiently.

He stopped and pushed open the passenger door while she slipped her sandal back on.

"What took you so long?" she asked.

To his disappointment, she had unrolled her waistband, returning her skirt to its previous length.

"I had to make sure he wasn't still watching at the window before I started the car."

She smiled as if flattered that anyone would do such a thing, and Hunter wondered if she knew just how powerful an effect she had on men.

"I don't know whether to clobber you or kiss you for what you just did," Hunter added.

She ducked her head and gave a bashful grin. "Do I get a choice?"

Hunter felt himself react physically to her suggestion, then struggled to focus on the matter at hand. "No, same as you didn't have the choice to come out here and interfere with my surveillance."

Lifting her chin and raising her eyebrows, she shot him a knowing look. "Interfere? Tell me, how long had you been stalking that guy?"

"I told you, it's not stalking. I had been observing him for three days."

"And how long did it take to get your evidence after I showed up, hmm?" She lifted her arm and looked at her watch. "About three minutes. Let this be a lesson," she said smugly. "It pays to tap into a woman's intuition."

"There are procedures...." Hunter took a calming breath. "Procedures that you broke to smithereens."

"Yeah, like those procedures were getting you anywhere," she scoffed. "When are you going to loosen up? There aren't always right and wrong ways of doing things, merely different ways."

Gritting his teeth, he turned away from her and her confused logic and put the car in gear. "What brought you out here this afternoon?"

"I told you. Woman's intuition."

Julie caught the look of frustration he shot her and decided it would be a good move to tell him how she had arrived at her plan. "Actually, the clues were already in Younce's file. His police record shows a history of getting into fights at bars, and his wages are being garnished for child support for four kids by as many mothers. So I put two and two together and figured that Younce likes women." She brushed her hands together. "So I provided the bait that I knew he would take and, voilà! Case closed."

Hunter narrowed his eyes at her as if she were somehow the guilty party. She folded her arms over her chest. *Ingrate!*

"You've got to admit I was a big help today." Given the fierceness of his scowl, she was probably pushing her luck. But Julie didn't care. Unable to stand another day of paperwork tedium, she was willing to risk his wrath as long as she got away from that awful desk. "So, what's our next case going to be?"

He made a sound that approached a growl, then mindlessly ran a thumb over the scar at the corner of his mouth. She waited a moment while he shifted gears and drove past her parked vehicle.

"Hey, that's my car. Aren't you going to let me out?"

"You can get it later. But first you're going to help me find the mystery kisser."

"This monster is a gas hog," Julie announced. "You really ought to trade it in for a car that's more environment friendly."

Hunter flexed his hand on the steering wheel. "Just keep your eye on Anna's taillights."

They were several vehicles behind the Volvo when it went through the exact-change tollgate. Hunter took a shorter line and cut some of the distance between them.

"Aren't you worried about what you might find?" Julie tugged the seat belt away from her neck. "What if something you uncover causes even more problems between your brother and his wife? Wouldn't you feel guilty?''

He turned and looked over his shoulder before switching lanes. ''My job is to find the truth. If Anna has betrayed Pete, then she deserves whatever consequences the truth may bring.''

Julie felt her stomach muscles clench. When her own betrayal came to light, it was doubtful he'd be any less harsh with her. For a moment, she considered telling him that Anna was not the mystery kisser. But what good would that do? He wouldn't believe her unless he knew the identity of the real mystery kisser. And if she told him *that*, then she may as well kiss her reporting job goodbye.

With any luck, Anna's activities were completely innocent and no harm would come of their following her. But in the meantime, how much would Hunter learn about the mystery kisser? And would he discover Julie's alter ego before she had a chance to prove herself as a journalist?

They followed the yellow Volvo onto the downtown exit ramp and east toward the Shockoe district. When Anna pulled into the Shockoe Slip, a tiny cul-de-sac with a decorative fountain in the center of the loop of pavement, Hunter parked along Main Street, diagonally across from her car. Not actually a street, since it led nowhere, the Slip sat like a cloistered witness to the boisterous Friday-night activity on Main Street. Julie and Hunter watched for a moment while Anna pulled down her lighted visor and re-touched her makeup.

''By the way, you're welcome for helping you nab Younce today.'' Julie paused. ''So maybe now you'll agree that I'm more useful as a surveillance partner than as a secretary.''

He slanted a wicked smile at her. ''I would've gotten him anyway. There was a twenty-dollar bill lying on the sidewalk.''

''Now *that* really would have been obvious. While you were at it, why didn't you just put up a sign? Smile, you're on *Candid Camera*.'' She peered into the car at him and got the distinct impression that he was just messing with her mind. ''Even if you had put the money there, it must have blown away, because I didn't see any sign of it.''

His grin grew, and she knew she'd been right about him.

''Then you'd better work on your powers of observation,'' he said with a chuckle.

Anna finished her primping and consulted a slip of paper as if checking the address.

Julie sighed. She was glad to be here—glad to be helping Hunter on an actual case—but sleuthing offered her even fewer opportunities to meet and kiss a hundred men than the office work had. Taking her eyes off their prey for a moment, she studied Hunter's face in the eerie glow of the streetlight. The cut of his features was every bit as intense as the man himself. Chin handsomely squared and covered with a day's-end shadow of beard. Nose sharp and firm. Ears artfully curved and begging her to nibble their lobes. And eyes rimmed with lashes and brows so black and thick they seemed to melt into the night.

Wishful thinking led her to try to justify seeking one hundred kisses rather than one hundred men. Given a choice, she'd prefer to collect the remaining kiss samples from Hunter alone.

He lifted his arm and pointed toward the Slip. "She's getting out of the car." Giving Julie's arm a little push, he told her, "Go down there and see where she's heading."

"Me? Don't you want to go, too?" Now that she had the opportunity to play spy, she was worried about making a mistake.

"Yes, you. She might recognize me." He reached across her, his thick arm brushing her waist, and opened her door. The door lights had been covered with duct tape, and all except for the streetlight on the other side of the fountain remained dark. "Now, go!"

In her haste, Julie practically tumbled out of the car. Hoping the commotion hadn't attracted Anna's attention, she forced herself to stroll sedately into the circular drive. Fortunately, the older woman seemed so intent on her destination that she looked neither left nor right as she passed in front of the fountain.

Julie glanced back at Hunter, but he motioned for her to keep her attention on the subject. Farther down Main Street, toward the clubs and restaurants, Friday-night revelers shouted greetings to one another. Julie tugged her skirt down a fraction of an inch and carefully picked her way along the cobblestone drive, all the while hoping she didn't look like a streetwalker trying to pick up a customer.

Pretending no interest in the woman ahead of her, Julie loitered by the fountain while Anna disappeared into the tall building at the center of the Slip. As soon as she was inside, Julie ran up to the stoop and peered in through the glass doors, but saw no one. The only hint that anyone had been there was the red glow of the number 2 above the elevator.

She tried the door, but it was locked. On the left side of the building, a decorative ivy trellis rose to just beneath the second-floor window. The thin, wooden structure was secured with something that looked like green pipe cleaners, but at five feet two inches, and barely topping a hundred pounds, Julie doubted she'd present more weight than it could support.

Kicking off her shoes, she walked through a bed of smooth pebbles, hoisted herself onto the lowest crosspiece and grabbed a handful of ivy and trellis higher up. The wood creaked. What worried her more than how much weight the thing would hold was how many spiders might be hiding in the greenery.

Wrinkling her nose, she pushed that unpleasant thought aside and focused on the fact that this was her chance to prove to Hunter that she had what it took to be his co-detective. Spiders or not, this was still a heck of a lot better than typing. And who knew? Maybe someday she'd be able to tell her grandchildren about the time she was a lady detective. Or was it detectress?

Julie was more than halfway up when something went *sproing* and the trellis shook under her. Then the whole thing swayed outward, away from the building. Startled, she tried to jerk herself closer, but the movement merely added momentum to the popping of pipe cleaners all around her.

She felt herself falling backward, and stiffened for the inevitable impact. When a pair of strong hands closed around her waist, Julie let out a muffled shriek. In the next moment, two bodies tumbled against the loose pebbles. Julie's crash was cushioned by a warm male torso.

"Ooohhh." A deep moan came from beneath her.

Mustering as much grace and dignity as circumstances would allow, Julie rolled over and peered into the pained face of her long-suffering employer. "Hunter, are you all right?"

She knelt beside him and rested a hand on his chest. *Mmm, nice.* Taking her hand in his, he moved it to his waist and spoke with effort.

"I think I may have bruised a rib or two." He moaned again. "Or maybe six."

"Oh, no. Do you want me to call an ambulance?"

"Sure," he wheezed, "and while you're at it, why don't you hire a marching band and a team of jugglers? Anything to draw more attention to ourselves."

He eased himself up to a sitting position and probed his chest as if to determine the extent of his injuries. Although he winced twice, he seemed satisfied that nothing was broken, and rose slowly to his feet.

"Well, you don't have to be snippy about it," she said, slipping her shoes back on and following him to the fountain. Hunter stood with his back to the fish sculpture that arched above the stone-and-concrete edifice. Julie would have suggested he sit down on the fountain's basin rim and catch his breath, but his annoyed expression told her he would not be receptive to her show of concern. "It wasn't like I *asked* you to be under me when the trellis collapsed."

"I was trying to keep you from killing yourself," he said, flexing both hands, "and I almost ended up getting killed myself."

She craned her neck to look up at him. Even if his size weren't so intimidating, that scowl would be enough to send a lesser person running for cover.

"What, pray tell, were you doing on the trellis? Besides making enough noise to alert half the neighborhood to your presence, that is."

"You told me to follow her. The front door was locked, so I..." Julie gestured behind her toward the side wall, where the trellis sagged outward, and the ivy seemed to be groping the air with its broken vines.

"I told you to watch her."

"And that's what I planned to do once I reached the second-story window!"

"Shh!" He touched a finger to his lips. "Let's just wait here. It may be awhile before she comes back out."

"Aren't you concerned about being recognized?"

"If she comes out, we'll act like business associates."

"At nine-thirty on a Friday night?" As if to confirm her words, a club door opened halfway down the block on Main, and music spilled out into the street. "It would be more believable if we act like a couple out for a romantic stroll after a few drinks at O'Leary's Pub."

Taking his hand in hers, she leaned close and fluttered her eyelashes at him like a besotted schoolgirl. Julie experienced an instant of triumph when his Adam's apple bobbed as he swallowed hard, then he sat abruptly on the edge of the fountain.

"Do you think we should try to find a way into the building to see what Anna's doing?" Julie patted her waist as if checking for a pocket. "I have a credit card somewhere."

Hunter started to rise. "You're not going to get anywhere with a—"

Behind her, a latch clicked and the door squeaked open.

"It's Anna," he said, and tried to straighten the rest of the way.

Julie was still holding his hand. Afraid that any further movement on his part would only call attention to them, she grasped his wrist with her other hand and pushed downward, hoping he'd stay seated and she could shield his face with her body. With the streetlight shining directly toward him, there was no question his sister-in-law would recognize him as she returned to her car.

His center of gravity already at a precarious point, Julie's instinctive reaction sent Hunter sprawling backward, legs pedaling in the air as he tried to right himself. Horrified as his hand slipped from her grasp, she could only watch helplessly as he made a loud splashdown in the fountain.

Hunter's subsequent sputtering and floundering only made matters worse. The drenched white cotton shirt lay glued to his chest in a way that almost made Julie forget about Anna completely, as her imagination went wild.

Reluctantly, she pulled her thoughts back to the present. With a quick glance over her shoulder, Julie saw that Anna, her brows creased in worry, had indeed noticed their activity and was headed toward them with the clear intent of offering assistance.

Thinking quickly, Julie let out an excited whoop of laughter reminiscent of some of the party-goers up the block. "Honey-doll, I *tol'* you not to have those last three drinks!"

Then, faking an inebriated enthusiasm, she flung herself into the fountain after Hunter. The cold water momentarily sucked the breath from her lungs. In an effort to block his face from the curious woman approaching them, Julie plastered herself to him, from hip to chest...to lips.

As their mouths met, Hunter instantly ceased his struggling. Instead, his arms encircled her waist, pressing her to him in a way that proved the cold water was having no effect on him.

Mindless of the sodden shirt clinging to her hardened nipples, or the faux suede skirt that had ridden up so far she was surely displaying the lace edge of her undies, Julie heeded only the heat and passion that seemed to rise like steam from the man under her.

As his mouth slid from her lips and trailed to the hollow beneath her ear, Julie was only vaguely aware of a woman's surprised gasp and the rapid staccato of retreating footsteps across the cobbles before a car started up and sped away.

Sliding one hand down Julie's back, Hunter clutched a crescent of bare flesh that peeked from beneath her panties, and urged her ever closer as his lips covered hers, breathing warmth into her mouth and into her soul.

With immense effort, she sought to catch her breath and return to reason. When words finally came, they were barely a whisper. "She's gone.... We can stop kissing now."

"Mmm," Hunter responded.

His lips made a foray down to the soggy V of her

shirt, and Julie inhaled so sharply the sound seemed to echo in the secluded cul-de-sac. When his tongue dipped beneath her neckline to the soft curve of her breast, she wanted only to remove the clinging barricade to their desire. And when his palm covered the lace panties, stroking her in a way that drove her wild with longing, her body ached for release from this beautiful torture.

A shiver shook her body.

Hunter looked up at her with glazed eyes, proving that he, too, had been affected by their moment of unplanned togetherness. Then he lifted a hand to her gooseflesh-covered arm. "You're freezing," he said. "Let's get out of here."

Dazed and reluctant, Julie stepped out of the shallow pool, the cool evening breeze slapping her back to her senses. Her breathing came in ragged gasps, but she wasn't sure whether it was because of the temperature or her physical reaction to Hunter.

She turned to wait for him while he plucked her shoes out of the fountain and handed them to her. Gratefully accepting his warm arm around her shoulders, she walked with him back to the car.

"You know," he said as they stepped from the cobblestones onto the sidewalk, "whenever you're around, nothing ever goes according to plan."

Chapter Five

Adventurous circumstances seem to heighten the excitement of kissing. What makes the act of osculation even more titillating is the risk of getting caught.

Hunter stood at the door of Julie's town house apartment. The neighborhood, a pleasant complex that catered mostly to singles and retirees, was not far from where they'd grown up. He lifted his arm to rap the brass knocker, and cringed when his ribs protested the movement.

She appeared a moment later, dressed in shorts. Her hair was held back by a tie-dyed scarf, and a dust rag dangled from her hand. Her freckles seemed to glow as if she'd just finished polishing them. "Your timing's perfect. I just finished my Saturday cleanup chores."

A laugh escaped his throat. "My, how times have

changed. I seem to recall you hiding at my house whenever Gran got out the feather duster and hair scarf.''

Times had changed. Now *he* wanted to run home and avoid what he had come here for. But as much as he hated to admit it, her method for getting Younce to show himself physically sound yesterday had been quite effective. Perhaps they could team up again to close the Erol case.

She pulled the door open. "Won't you come in?"

An elderly neighbor across the parking lot came out and shook a rug over her porch rail. She seemed more interested in them than in her spring-cleaning.

"Sure." Once inside, he blurted out the purpose of his unannounced visit. "Wayne Erol, over on Oakview Road, has been on worker's comp for over a month due to an on-the-job knee injury. His ex-wife, who's mad about missing her alimony check because of it, informed his employer that she heard he's been dancing at nightclubs."

Hunter pushed a hand through his hair and hoped he wasn't making a mistake by asking Julie to accompany him again. Convincing himself it was to close the case so he could focus on his sister-in-law's activities, he refused to acknowledge the bigger reason—that he enjoyed Julie's company.

"I thought you might want to go with me to his house and drop your keys again. Just like yesterday."

She pulled the scarf off her head, and wavy brown tendrils fell over her shoulders. Hunter wanted to tangle his fingers in that luxurious mane, but after his response in the fountain last night, he thought it best to try to rein in such urges.

"I can't guarantee it will be exactly like the

Younce case," she warned. "That just happened sort of spontaneously. I have to get a 'read' on the subject and then go with the flow."

Hunter rolled his eyes. Physically, she had changed a lot over the years, but she was still just as exasperating as ever. "It will go according to plan as long as you pay close attention."

He outlined the plan for her, essentially summarizing exactly what had happened yesterday.

"But we've done it that way before."

"Right, and it works."

"I keep telling you, there's more than one way to skin a knee, but you always want to do the same-ole, same-ole."

Hunter could have argued that she was totally different from the women he was usually attracted to, which blew her "same-ole" theory, but such a confession would be unplanned, and therefore imprudent.

Her blue eyes pleaded with him to reconsider and let her run wild with this case, as she had done with the last two. Considering the near havoc she had wrought on them—as well as his heart rate—he steeled his expression and his resolve.

"'Same-ole' gets the job done, so I'll stick with that."

Julie sighed in annoyance and disappeared down the hall to put away her cleaning supplies. When she returned, her hair was freshly brushed and she was carrying the tiny black purse he'd seen at the office. And sneakers covered her previously bare feet.

"What kind of neighborhood does this Erol guy live in?"

Hunter shrugged. "Working-class. Decent, but nothing fancy."

She turned on her heel and disappeared again, returning with a flowered, open-weave satchel that had seen more prosperous days.

"That is the ugliest pocketbook I have ever seen."

Her answer was a savvy grin and a saucy tilt of her chin. "You watch. It may come in very handy."

"Just follow the plan," he said, and steered her out the door toward his car.

"Fuddy-duddy," Julie said over her shoulder.

A few minutes later they entered a tidy suburban neighborhood of small brick-and-frame ranchers. Hunter parked in front of a house two doors down from the Erol residence.

He squinted through his sunglasses and studied the scene. The place could use a fresh coat of paint, but the shrubs bordering the front of the house sported a recent trim. The asphalt-paved driveway ended in a wide apron at the top of a shallow slope, serving dual purpose as a basketball court for the net secured above it on a small garden shed. In the middle of the unfenced front yard sat two lawn chairs separated by a small table holding two canned drinks. A woman in shorts and a midriff top occupied one. A man—presumably Wayne Erol—rose from the other, dropped a kiss on her forehead and went inside the house.

Hunter grinned. The guy hadn't shown any sign of pain or stiffness. Hunter positioned the camera on the dashboard and handed Julie a street map to make her request for directions a bit more convincing. "Go for it."

Julie took the map but made no move to leave the car. "The plan isn't going to work. That woman—"

"It's okay, he'll be back outside in a minute," Hunter assured her. "No man seeing two women puzzling over a map can resist putting in his two cents' worth."

Disregarding his sexist comment, Julie grabbed the video camera and stuffed it into her purse. Adjusting the torn flowered liner around the lens, she was satisfied that the pink mesh over the rest of the bag camouflaged the spy instrument. Feeling immensely pleased with herself, she reached over and gave Hunter a light kiss on the cheek. "Our plan has changed."

"No. Put the camera back. We're sticking to the script."

"Just pretend you're my husband," she said, ignoring his protest. "Follow my lead."

Leaving the map on the floor of the car, Julie slung the bag over her shoulder and scooted out the door before he could stop her. She had crossed half the distance to the Erol yard when it appeared Hunter wasn't going to accompany her. Well, she could be stubborn, too! Turning around, she beckoned to him and called loudly enough for the neighbors to hear, "Come on, honey, let's take a look around."

When he finally joined her, she led them straight to the woman in the lawn chair. "Hi, I'm Julie..." She paused, wondering if detectives ever give their real names. "...Hokes. And this is my husband, Hunter."

"Yeah, Hunter Hoax," he said, and squeezed Julie's arm. The ponytailed woman rose from her chair, but appeared not to notice the irony of their made-up name.

"We saw a couple of houses for sale around here and were wondering about the neighborhood."

Hunter just looked at Julie, bug-eyed, and said nothing. The screen door opened, and their subject, apparently curious, walked smoothly to the front yard. Still no sign of a limp.

"I'm Cindy-Marie Madden, and this is my boyfriend, Wayne Erol."

Warming up to her role, Julie made small talk, chattering on about wanting to start a family and raise their children in a safe neighborhood near a good school. Obviously unaccustomed to playing it by ear, Hunter said little. But despite his silence, she could tell he was furious with her for coloring outside the lines. She adjusted the purse on her shoulder, an unspoken promise that he would get the evidence he sought.

Cindy-Marie allowed her gaze to scan the length of the street. "It's not upscale like that overpriced Bramblethorn subdivision, but people like us—" she gestured from herself to Julie "—appreciate a good bargain when we find one."

"I know what you mean." Julie lowered her voice and patted the frayed purse. "I got this bag at a half-off sale, and it's still going strong."

With a womanly bond now forged between them, Cindy-Marie nodded agreement. Julie shot Hunter a smug smile, to which he responded with an annoyed glare. Seeing his male impatience mirrored in Wayne's eyes, she decided now was a good time to move on to the next step—getting their subject to incriminate himself.

Sweeping an arm toward the garden shed, she said with a sigh, "That basketball hoop brings back happy memories. Hunter was on the high school basketball team, and I used to love to watch him play."

For the first time since he'd come outside, Wayne seemed to take an interest in his unexpected visitors. "Really?"

"Uh, I wasn't first-string or anything." Hunter's discomfort with the lie was easily mistaken for modesty.

"Wanna go a game of one-on-one?" Wayne asked.

Hunter hesitated, and Julie gave him a little nudge. "I haven't played in years," he confessed.

"Men!" Julie declared to Wayne's girlfriend. "They think they have to be perfect at everything." Hunter shot her a glance that proved her words had found their mark. It was a fact that he often tried so hard for perfection that he couldn't seem to enjoy the moment.

"Good," Wayne said with a grin, "then maybe we should make a friendly wager."

"You go ahead," Cindy-Marie urged good-naturedly. "We'll stay here and talk about you."

As the men made their way to the modest court, the women each took a seat on a lawn chair, and Julie carefully set her purse on the small table. Uncertain whether the camera was aimed properly, she dug around in the bag under the pretext of finding her sunglasses, and checked the small viewing screen. Perfect! To her relief, the mesh covering did not seem to hamper the visibility at all.

They watched in companionable silence as the men challenged each other, feigning left, then darting right. And not once did Wayne Erol limp or otherwise favor his knee. Twisting, turning and leaping, they fought for control of the ball, all the while pushing their bodies and straining their muscles in a show of manly competition.

It was a beautiful sight to behold. A short while into the game, action stopped, then resumed again after they took off their sweaty shirts. Pectorals flexed, biceps bunched and washboards rolled. Although Wayne worked in a warehouse and Hunter had an office job, Julie was surprised to discover that her boss was the more fit of the two men. Taller and heavier, he was also firmer and more sharply defined.

If possible, Julie was almost as turned on as she'd been last night in the fountain. A wistful sigh broke the silence, and Julie realized Cindy-Marie had been admiring her "husband," too.

"Have mercy," the other woman breathed. "Does he kiss as good as he looks?"

Julie leaned back in the chair and felt the sun warm her face. "You betcha."

He should have known she wouldn't be able to stick to the plan. They were sitting in the parking lot in front of her apartment, and Hunter debated whether to walk her to the door or just do a drop-and-run. A movement in his rearview mirror showed that the neighbor was now watering pots of begonias that hung from her porch.

"I'm sorry I forgot about your ribs. If I had remembered, I never would have suggested you shoot hoops." Julie easily folded the street map, a feat he'd rarely been able to accomplish, and returned it to his glove compartment. "Please come in and cool off before you drop from the heat."

He would probably regret it, but he followed her in anyway. This time, he took the opportunity to notice the eclectic decor in her apartment. A curious blend of light and dark woods, patterns and solids, and silver and brass, the pieces seemed to reflect many varying moods. The place was tidy, but a few small things out of their assigned areas made it look lived in. Yesterday's paper rested on the blue-and-green plaid sofa, and three shoes predictably remained where she had kicked them. The apartment looked like a comfortable place to come home to. And the most intriguing aspect of the place was its occupant.

"Other than your sore ribs, you have to admit today's events turned out pretty well," she bragged. Taking his hand, she led him toward the hall. "Come to the bedroom with me."

Hunter blinked and followed her to a room that seemed as mixed as the rest of the place. Frilly ruffles on the bedcover were balanced by a sedate, almost masculine dresser and nightstand. The pieces seemed as incongruous as the woman herself.

She'd always been a spontaneous sort, but this sure beat all. He wondered if his ribs could handle the stress. Worse, could his heart handle it if, tomorrow, she just as spontaneously decided she wanted nothing more to do with him?

Crossing the room ahead of him, she went to her doily-topped dresser and yanked open a drawer. First pulling out a silken nightie and mere scraps of underclothes, she tossed the stuff aside until she came to an oversize T-shirt.

"Here," she said, tossing it to him. "You'll be more comfortable in a clean shirt."

As the breath escaped from his chest in a whoosh, Hunter was both disappointed and relieved. He sat on the bed and stared at the limp garment in his lap.

He had no business wishing for things that weren't meant to be. His life had been scheduled into a comfortable—if not exhilarating—regimen, and Julie's unpredictability threw his carefully laid plans into turmoil. Hunter needed to know what to expect from day to day and minute to minute. Ever since her arrival, however, things seemed to change on a second's notice.

It wasn't that he didn't want a social life or a woman to share it with. Until a couple of weeks ago, he'd enjoyed quiet dates with women he'd chosen for their tranquil natures. Although none of them had stirred his soul, he was convinced that with time and patience he would someday find the right one. A peaceful woman who was calm, composed and serene.

The exact opposite of Julie Beth Fasano. He looked up and found her studying him with concern.

"Still sore, huh? Here, let me help you."

Standing before him, she lifted the hem of his Polo shirt…and his libido along with it. Strangely enough, the exercise this morning may have actually helped, because the soreness he felt now was only a mild twinge. But he enjoyed the view that her knit top offered him as he mutely lifted his arms for her to pull the fabric over his head. And his mutinous body urged him to return the favor.

Hunter reached out, his hands settling on her slim waist. A lifetime ago, when he had touched her like this, it was to boost her up into her new tree house. Too impatient to wait for the ladder rungs to be nailed to the tree trunk, the young tomboy had insisted on exploring it right away. With or without his consent.

Now Hunter understood that impatience, as he wanted to explore this mind-boggling woman standing before him. She stared down at him and rested her small hands on his shoulders. Her fingers trailed gently over his bare skin, down to his chest and then tentatively to the ridges at his sides.

Standing, he closed the distance between them. Her pale blue eyes gazed at him with trust and openness, leaving no question that she shared his hunger. Hunter touched the gold-streaked brown hair that tumbled from a side part and caressed her face before falling to her bare collarbone. Pushing the soft locks behind her shoulder, he then nudged the narrow strap of her top off her shoulder and dropped a kiss on the spot where it had rested.

Her head tipped back, inviting him to explore further. For once he was glad to abandon his plans for the day in order to see what surprises would reveal themselves in the uncharted moments that lay ahead. As he folded his arms around her, he savored the feel of her small body curved against his own.

Predictably unpredictable, Julie hesitantly disengaged from the embrace and moved to the window. Though she was still close enough for him to reach out and touch, it felt like a chasm gaped between them.

Her eyes still heavy-lidded with desire, she grasped the blind cord. "If we're going to do this," she said softly, "the blinds need to be closed. There's a nosy neighbor across the street."

When she returned to him, mere seconds had passed, but it was long enough for the fog in Hunter's mind to clear slightly. As much as he wanted to throw discretion aside and follow his impulses, reason ruled once again. The practical side of his brain took charge, reminding him that if he were to disregard his better judgment, it would only leave confusion and chaos in the wake of their lovemaking. Besides, after years of protecting Julie from her own rash decisions, he could not bring himself to take advantage of her impulsive personality.

"As much as I'd like to," he said, returning the stringlike strap to her shoulder, "I shouldn't."

She dropped her gaze with an expression of disappointment. Or was it embarrassment? Gosh, he hoped not.

"Of course. I should have remembered." Lifting the clean T-shirt to drop it over his head, she said, "You're still in a lot of pain."

"Yeah," he agreed, "it hurts." But he wasn't talking about his chest. He touched her arm. "I'm sorry."

Sorry for what he'd been about to do. Sorry that they were too different to find a way to make things work.

"That's okay. Don't worry about it." She smiled, and the room seemed to brighten despite the closed blinds. "Come on, let's go take a look at the film we shot this morning."

Leave it to her to go so steadily with the flow.

Back in the living room, she pushed her sneakers off, sat on the couch and patted the seat next to her.

Hunter sat down and tried not to be distracted by the fresh scent of her perfume. As she dug into her purse for the camera, he helped pull the tacky pink fabric away from it. A moment later, the tiny view-finder screen offered an image of two men dueling for control of the basketball.

He smiled. "It was worth losing the bet to get this film." Impulsively, he gave her knee an appreciative pat. "And you are definitely the queen of spontane-ity. I thought for sure you were going to blow our cover when you made up that phony name, but ev-erything turned out great."

"It was exciting, wasn't it?"

She squirmed with glee, and Hunter was reminded anew of their dunking in the fountain last night. He would have loved to give her a reason to squirm again.

"Maybe I'm a secret daredevil, but the risk of get-ting caught made it even more fun for me. When I told them our name was Hokes, it was like walking on the edge of a cliff, waiting to see if they fell for it."

A twinge of recognition reverberated at the back of Hunter's mind. He frowned, trying to remember why her words sounded so familiar.

"What? Didn't you enjoy it, too?"

"I could have used a little less excitement."

She laughed and jostled his arm. "Fuddy-duddy! Where's your sense of adventure?"

Adventure...that was it. Her sentiments almost ex-actly mirrored the mystery kisser's recent column. Narrowing his eyes, he studied the face that seemed so guileless and innocent. Could Julie's quest for adventure have led her to write about her romantic escapades for the entire city to read?

No, he thought, dismissing the idea as ludicrous. Julie as the mystery kisser? What were the odds of that? Or of his sister-in-law being the columnist, either. Where Anna was concerned, his efforts were mostly geared toward ruling her out as the anonymous reporter.

As for his momentary flight of imagination regarding Julie, Hunter chalked it up to a moment of paranoia. Julie had a way of setting him off balance, and today was no exception. The only thing he could expect from her with any reliability, he was discovering, was that she always did the unexpected.

Glancing at the calendar on his watch, he calculated that it was still three weeks before his secretary was due to return. And with her would come the peace and order that he craved.

He only hoped he could hold out until then.

"I need you to change Mrs. Ingram's appointment from Thursday afternoon to Friday at ten." Hunter dropped the note and a folder on the desk, which was starting to look normal in its state of disarray. "Then print out the new schedule for the week and bring it to my office."

Julie had turned down the volume on her radio, but he could tell she was more interested in listening to the *Burning Issues* program than fulfilling his request.

"Uh, I haven't learned how to do that."

"It's easy," he said, bending over her to call up the appointment program on her computer screen.

"It's a WYSIWYG program, so all you have to do is point and click."

The radio deejay informed them he would return after the commercial break and air some callers' guesses as to the mystery kisser's identity.

"What? She wears a frizzy wig?"

Hunter stifled a sigh. "WYSIWYG," he said, raising his voice to hold her fleeting attention. "What you see is what you get. It means that whatever appears on the screen is exactly how the schedule will print out."

"Oh." Clearly, this wasn't adventurous enough to elicit any enthusiasm on her part.

"You need to familiarize yourself with our computer research procedures, because I'd like for you to work on the mystery kisser case," he said, and gave her the file he'd brought in with him. Anna's name had been handwritten on the tab, and a red Personal and Confidential sticker shouted from the front of the folder.

Julie practically ejected herself from the chair as she rose from her slouched position. Her efforts at surveillance on the faked-injury cases had been grudgingly accepted by Hunter and reluctantly acknowledged as helpful. The last thing she expected was for him to turn over portions of a case that was so close to him personally. "Me?"

"Yes, you convinced me that there may be something to this 'woman's intuition' you spoke of."

Good grief, when would she learn to keep her mouth shut? "You mean, you want me to get pictures or something?"

"Heavens, no." Hunter chuckled and shot her a wink, as if she should somehow understand his sudden humor. "I'm not ready to turn you loose on Anna or some other poor, unsuspecting person. What I want you to do is pursue all the paper trails that may lead to her. I'll give you a list of places to start—Anna's bank accounts and credit transactions should help give us a fix on whether she might be the one—and if you can think of any other possibilities you can trace them, too."

Okay, so he wasn't ready to send Julie out on her own yet, but she must have earned a small measure of his trust for him to pass such an important project on to her.

She bit her bottom lip. On one hand, his request was perfect in that it would allow her to intercept any information that might bring him too close to the mystery kisser's true identity. But on the other hand, it placed her smack in the middle of an ethical dilemma. Her experience had always been that honesty was the best policy, and Hunter was even more of a stickler for the complete and unadulterated truth. Julie considered sliding past this one on the technicality that withholding the truth wasn't actually a lie, but her conscience urged her to do the right thing and come clean.

"Look, I don't think it's such a good idea for me to work on this particular case."

"Where's your sense of adventure?" Hunter retorted, goading her. "Don't you want to find the mystery kisser before you leave the firm? You might even win the radio contest."

Adventure…that's what this whole thing had started as. But now things were getting too complicated. She had never intended to deceive her friend or otherwise betray his trust. If she told him now—

after allowing him to believe that his sister-in-law might be the culprit—that she herself was the author of the column, her job here would end immediately. And Julie wouldn't blame Hunter for putting her out on the street.

She had to break her promise to the editor and tell Hunter the truth, even though it meant trusting him to keep her secret and not turn her in to the radio station so he could use the opportunity to advertise his agency. She had helped him catch two people who'd been trying to defraud his client, the insurance company, so he at least owed her that.

The jingle signaling the beginning of the *Burning Issues* segment came on the radio. Hunter reached over and nudged the volume up.

He didn't owe her a job. With any luck, she might get employment as a waitress to take the place of this temporary gig. Such a position would even provide her with plenty of kissable men to add to her list. But she wouldn't enjoy that job—or the boss—as much as she did this one.

"Actually, I need to talk to—"

"Shh!" He turned the sound up another notch.

The caller's voice came through despite the cell phone static. "Is the mystery kisser that lady warden over at the jailhouse? Her name is Ann Onchman." He wasn't the first caller to go on a fishing expedition based on clues as slim as their sharing first names. The deejay paused for a long moment, prompting the man to add, "You gotta admit, her name is real close, and she'd sure have plenty of opportunities for kissing."

The radio announcer laughed hysterically at the implication that the warden would be kissing the

BUSINESS REPLY MAIL

FIRST-CLASS MAIL   PERMIT NO. 717-003   BUFFALO, NY

POSTAGE WILL BE PAID BY ADDRESSEE

SILHOUETTE READER SERVICE
3010 WALDEN AVE
PO BOX 1867
BUFFALO NY 14240-9952

NO POSTAGE
NECESSARY
IF MAILED
IN THE
UNITED STATES

prisoners. "That's about the wildest guess I've heard yet!"

"It's ridiculous, that's what it is." Julie turned the radio off, garnering a censuring frown from Hunter. Although she'd originally appreciated the publicity generated by the column, now she was wondering if it wasn't too much of a good thing. "This has turned into a witch-hunt, and innocent Anns, Annies and even Annabelles are getting unwanted attention because of it."

"You're right." Hunter squeezed the spare hand-grip he now kept at Julie's desk. "Let's hope no one remembers the judge's wife, also named Anna, took creative writing courses in college."

His handsome features drew together in a look of genuine concern. The least she could do was put his mind at ease about Anna…and trust that he would keep her confidence. The thrill over the risk of getting caught was wearing thin, and she was ready to own up to her role in the mystery. "Hunter, I believe I can help you—"

"Actually, you can help if you know how to play tennis."

"Yes, I do, but—"

"Good, bring your outfit to wear tomorrow."

"But I don't have one."

"Then dip into petty cash and buy one." He reached into the drawer, withdrew a small lockbox and handed her some bills. "There's a carpal tunnel case who has reserved a tennis court for tomorrow afternoon, and we're going to be there."

Julie sat there dumbly, holding the cash, as she considered her options. Telling him she was the mystery kisser was the right thing to do. And she *would* tell him. Soon. But if she spilled the beans now, he'd fire her before she had a chance to help him with this latest case. The least she could do was wait until after tomorrow's tennis game.

"Do you want me to bring my flowered purse to hold the video camera?"

Hunter reached back into the cash box and pushed some more bills into her hand. "This will be at a nice health club. Get something tasteful."

Chapter Six

It has been said that kisses never lie. Whether he wants it to or not, a man's personality is revealed by his kiss...which is why I'm conducting this survey and test. But what if the woman has something to hide? Does her kiss convey her deception and subsequent guilt? For now, at least, I hope not.

"That went well despite a few unexpected improvisations on your part," Hunter said as he gathered up their tennis rackets and balls.

Julie's first impulse was to rise to her defense with an explanation of why she had deviated from their script. But more pressing was the niggling sense of guilt that haunted her. "How do you do it?" she asked. "How do you resolve having to lie to people?"

Hunter bounced a lime-green ball on the ground

as the next players took their places on the court. "It's not really lying if your ultimate goal is to bring the truth to light," he said. "The first thing you have to do is take your heart out of it. You have to focus on the positive results rather than the means by which you get them." He caught the ball with a quick downward grab, then tossed it to her. "As long as you're not breaking any laws, you're in the clear."

He was right. She hadn't broken any laws. But she had betrayed his trust. And that fact was weighing heavily on her mind.

Julie peeled the plastic lid off the can and dropped the tennis ball inside. If she wanted to be successful in her job, both current and future, she would have to develop a thicker hide...and learn to put results before methods. In an effort to appease her guilt, she told herself she was acting, not lying, and that the experience would help her with her future reporting job.

"The important thing," Hunter continued, "is that we got them on videotape." He flashed her a genuine smile that she had difficulty returning.

"But I liked Mrs. Ramsey. She gave me her phone number and told me to keep in touch."

Hunter's gaze darkened. "She wasn't the only one passing along phone numbers."

He seemed angry, which was surprising considering his earlier satisfaction at having cinched this case.

"I thought you said the method didn't matter, as long as the desired results were achieved. So it shouldn't matter that I ditched the married act and let those guys give me their phone numbers."

Sheesh, what was his problem, anyway? As much

as she would have liked following through on the attraction that seemed to buzz between her and Hunter, he seemed almost to push her away at times. He was a man—virile, strong and proud—so his interest in her may have been merely physical. With Julie, it was that and much more. He excited her in a way that no man had ever done before. He stimulated her intellectually, he made her laugh at times—usually when he least intended it—and, despite their occasional moments of friction, she knew she could count on him in times of need. But the fact that he met all her needs and desires did not mean he felt the same about her. It seemed that he was trying to be exceedingly businesslike with her lately. With regret, Julie acknowledged that the remoteness was his way of telling her that there could never be anything more than a superficial friendship between them.

The two spectators had flirted with her when she had paused during the game to get a drink of water, so she had taken advantage of adding two more potential kissers to her list. But despite her relief over having new subjects to research and report upon, she couldn't work up any interest in calling either of them.

If she did pursue a meeting, the sole purpose would be to compare their kisses to Hunter's. But since she knew ahead of time who would come out on top, it seemed pointless to bother with them.

"If you want to continue going on assignments with me," Hunter warned, "you're going to have to stick to the established procedures."

"Right," she said with resigned complacency. "And deception is part of the procedure. Which makes it hard to call what we do an 'honest living.'"

Dejected, Julie picked up her purse with the camera carefully hidden inside and slowly headed toward the gate after the couple who had left before them.

Hunter's attitude softened as he fell into step beside her. "Not everyone is cut out for this line of work," he said gently. "If it bothers you this much, I won't ask you to come on assignments with me anymore."

"Please, no. I want to go spying with you." At his narrow-eyed glance, she amended her statement. "I mean, go on surveillance with you."

She hadn't meant to get herself taken off spy duty, but rather to resolve her guilt over doing it. The techniques she was learning—such as when Hunter passed himself off as his older brother and used Peter's membership pass to gain access to the club— were methods that might come in handy for stories she would report on later.

"I want to learn," she said, trying not to sound desperate. "I'll do anything you need me to."

Hunter paused and leaned against the chain-link fence near the gate. "Are you sure? Because I've decided to use you for some undercover work on the mystery kisser case, after all."

Julie rubbed the toe of her shoe against the asphalt. Now would be a good time to spill the truth. But if she did, how would she explain not having told him sooner? It seemed that the longer she waited, the harder it was becoming to break the silence.

"You can say no. I'll understand."

Now wasn't the time, she decided. Taking a deep breath, she wondered if the time would ever be right.

"It will involve more deception," she said, referring to her ongoing pretense with him. A pretense that, when eventually uncovered, would leave him feeling betrayed and mistrusted. She *would* tell him, she promised herself. But not now. Later, when the time was right. She tried not to linger on the thought that the time might never be right.

"Yes, it will. But I have faith that you'll come through. You won't let me down."

She hesitated long enough to garner a questioning gaze from Hunter. "I'll do it. Who knows, perhaps what I learn while working with you will help me in my next job."

He laughed at her supposed joke, then turned serious. "Then you'll need to follow my instructions precisely and remain invisible to the subject. Don't improvise like you did today."

Or the previous two times.

"It worked, didn't it? You *did* say it's important to focus on the positive results," she said, throwing his words back at him.

His lips tightened into a thin line before he grudgingly acknowledged that her impromptu suggestion had been successful. "You're right. Inviting the Ramseys to join us in a couples match after they'd finished their set extended her playing time. And that should prove without a doubt that Mrs. Ramsey's wrist is in perfect working order."

Julie handed him the videotape and took the camera out of her purse to put in a fresh cassette.

"But you still need to stick to the agency's procedures," he cautioned. "Next time we film a suspect, you should wait until we get back to the car before changing—"

The gate was flung open, and Mrs. Ramsey

launched herself at them with nails bared and hair flying.

Reacting instinctively, Hunter responded with his years of police and investigative training. As he quickly slid the taped evidence into his pocket, he automatically threw himself between the woman and Julie.

Although his maneuver prevented the enraged woman from harming Julie physically, it came too late to keep her from grabbing the camera and dashing it to the ground. Their cover had been blown, and Mrs. Ramsey was anything but happy.

It was too late to do anything about the expensive equipment, but Hunter was determined that she not take out her anger on Julie. The problem was that his temporary employee would not stay safely behind him, but kept popping out from one side or the other and peeking over his shoulder.

"How could you do this to me?" Mrs. Ramsey shrieked at her. "You little phony. I thought you were nice. I thought you were—" The steam suddenly went out of her boiler, and her posture crumpled as she covered her face with her hands and released a floodgate of supposedly heartfelt tears. Mrs. Ramsey lifted her face to Julie, showing two black mascara streaks coursing down her cheeks. When she spoke again, her voice was soft but strained. "I thought you were going to be my friend."

Hunter opened his arms in an attempt to keep Julie behind him. He had no doubt that, with a heart as soft as hers, she'd be swayed by the tears, regardless of their sincerity—or lack thereof.

But before he could stop her, she ducked under his elbow and went to the woman. Julie was crying even harder than Mrs. Ramsey, sobbing in remorse as she put her arms around the middle-aged woman's shoulders.

"I'm so sorry," she said. "I didn't mean to hurt you."

Never mind that the woman had brought it on herself by trying to swindle her employer and disability-insurance carrier. Mrs. Ramsey latched on to her guilt and gave her a kicked-puppy look. "You *lied* to me!"

Julie sniffed and reached into her purse for a tissue. "I know. And I feel terrible about having deceived you." She wiped her eyes, then blew into the tissue. "For what it's worth, I had a wonderful time playing tennis with you and your husband."

To Hunter's surprise, the other woman seemed heartened by Julie's indiscreet admission.

"At first it seemed fun to trick people so I could get what I wanted from them," Julie said, "but to tell you the truth, I don't think I'm cut out for deception and subterfuge. The guilt is killing me."

Subterfuge? He'd better get her out of here before her conscience prompted her to do something foolish.

"Please," Julie said, reaching out to touch the other woman's arm, "let me make it up to you."

"We have to go now," Hunter said, taking her elbow firmly in hand.

She jerked free of his grasp and turned back to face the woman, who was clearly pleased at having manipulated her emotions. Julie reached into her purse again and pulled out a videocassette.

"Here. Take this," she said, thrusting the case at her. "I couldn't live with myself, knowing that I had abused our friendship, no matter how brief it was."

Obviously stunned by Julie's foolhardy generosity, Mrs. Ramsey snatched it from her. "You did the right thing," the woman said, then quickly left, ignoring the water bottle she had come back to retrieve.

Julie gazed wistfully after the fleeing woman. "If we had met under different circumstances," she said, "we might have been good friends."

Hunter stepped closer and draped an arm around her shoulder. She was clearly shaken by the turn of today's events, and he wanted to comfort her with more than just a brotherly hug. But that could much too easily lead to a friendly kiss, which could lead to—

Impulsive reactions were Julie's forte. And since he was the older and more experienced of the two, it fell to him to draw safe, clear boundaries between them.

"About that videotape you gave her..."

Blotting a tear that had spilled over onto her freckled cheek, Julie said, "Yes?"

"That was the blank one."

She nodded and sniffed again. "I know."

A light burned in the living room, and two shadowy figures moved past the curtained window to settle on a sofa. Having watched Anna go in, Julie and Hunter knew for sure that one of the silhouettes was female. It was impossible to tell about the other, but Hunter had a sickening, gut-level hunch.

"What are you waiting for? Let's go peek."

The passenger door clicked open, and he instinctively grabbed Julie's arm to keep her from galloping up to the house. The hasty action caused the file of papers to fall from his lap into disarray around the gearshift. Hunter sighed. Once again her impulsive action had caused a mini-calamity. By now, experience had proved that scolding served no purpose when it came to Julie, but he couldn't help wondering aloud if he should have come alone tonight.

"Yeah, right," she said, handing him the last of the disorganized papers and stuffing them helter-skelter into the manila folder. "Just like you broke into Anna's house by yourself and wouldn't let me come with you."

She was scolding *him?*

"I didn't break in," he corrected. "Pete gave me the key. And my window of opportunity for going in while she went grocery shopping was so small that I didn't have time to call for backup." A smug expression of self-importance crossed Julie's face as she apparently interpreted herself to be the backup to which he referred, which compelled him to add, "Even if I had wanted to."

Rather than be offended by his bluntness, she redirected her attention to the printed contents of Anna's computer files. "How long did it take you to hack her password?"

He shrugged. "About twenty seconds. You'd be amazed how many people use the family dog's name."

A tiny, sheepish grin lifted her dark red lips ever so slightly. "Looks like I'll have to change mine first thing tomorrow."

Hunter reached over and touched her chin. "You don't have to worry about me looking through your files."

Julie briefly turned away from his touch and his gaze. Of course she wouldn't have to worry about him reading her files; she wrote all her newspaper columns on the computer at home. So why did she feel so exposed—so vulnerable—whenever she was around him? Uncomfortably aware that he was studying her, she sought to turn the focus away from herself and the secret she was withholding from him.

"I'm not worried, but your sister-in-law should be," she quipped. "What did you find that will help prove she's not the mystery kisser?"

Hunter's grip on the file tightened until, even in the deepening dusk, Julie could see the whitening of his knuckles.

"Actually, what I've read so far is pretty damning." He folded the tab down as if to lock the ugly contents inside. For a moment, the muscle in his jaw worked as he gazed fixedly at the house. Slapping the file against his knee, he gave a humorless laugh. "It's a miserable feeling to snoop into a family member's belongings. And even worse to find something like this."

A light rain fell, speckling the windshield and obscuring their view. Hunter reached for the key, as if deliberating whether to leave now before he discovered any new secrets involving his sister-in-law. His hand paused in midmotion before he changed his mind and lifted a pair of binoculars to his eyes.

"I know what you mean. It's hard for a person who's normally up front and open to operate this way." Julie leaned back in the seat and squinted through the rain at the couple on the sofa, who seemed to be engrossed in a book or something. "Sometimes you just have to weigh whether the end justifies the means."

When Hunter jerked his attention from the house

to scrutinize her, she realized he must have picked up on the autobiographical quality of her statement.

Julie reached for the folder and flipped it open with a nonchalance she didn't feel. ''So what exactly is in here?''

Hunter moved as if to take it from her, but she tucked the evidence between her hip and the door.

''Whatever you share with me stays with me,'' she assured him. ''I can keep a secret.'' Even if it meant hurting a friend, unfortunately. But Mr. Upshaw had insisted on her remaining anonymous—it was a condition of winning the job. No matter how close she had come recently to blurting out the truth to Hunter, there was no question that it would be best if she continued her silence for a while longer. At least until she got the columnist job. And then she'd be free to 'fess up.

It seemed as though he was trying to stare her down. Hunter's stern gaze reminded her of the time she'd accidentally broken the hand brake on his new bicycle when she'd borrowed it without his permission. Although she'd tried to pretend ignorance about the damage, he must have read the guilt in her eyes.

In order to avoid repeating that mistake, she pulled a clean tissue from her pocket and began wiping fog from the inside of the windshield. Quickly, before she was aware of what was happening, Hunter lunged forward and snatched the tissue from her grasp.

''Wha—?''

''You may as well be waving a flag,'' he said, tucking the soggy white paper into his shirt pocket. ''Here, use this instead.''

He handed her a dark flannel cloth cut from an old

shirt of his, and wondered, not for the first time, why he had invited her to come with him tonight. Experience told him it was because the hours went faster when he shared the time with another person. His head told him that staying alert to Julie's potential foibles would keep him from getting bored and falling asleep. But another part of his body told him it was because the enforced hours together offered opportunities to kiss or cuddle or...whatever. Not that he would or should allow such a thing to happen.

The ruler from south of the equator won the debate. Hunter handed her a miniature penlight. "Hold the rag over the light and paper so as not to attract attention."

She did as he suggested, and when the printed words sank in, the whites of her eyes threatened to serve as more of a flare than the tissue she'd waved earlier. "Oh, my!"

"That was my reaction, too," he admitted. "Only I didn't phrase it as delicately as you did."

He waited while she scanned the first couple of pages. Julie, as well as himself, had resisted the possibility that Anna might be the mystery kisser. But these documents appeared to be more than just circumstantial. The similarities between them and the mystery kisser's column were uncanny. And even if Anna was not the new columnist, her notes certainly led him—and anyone else with elementary powers of deduction—to believe that she was having an affair.

"You're not going to tell Peter, are you?"

"Of course I am. He asked me to find out the truth."

"But what if this isn't what it seems? You, of

all people, should know that appearances can be... deceiving.''

"Do you women always band together to defend each other?"

It was a joke, but she took him seriously. "No, it's not that. Suppose there's a legitimate reason for writing this stuff?''

And then he understood. Her guilt over having duped Mrs. Ramsey, whose company she had enjoyed while they played tennis, was spilling over into her role in discovering evidence that could ultimately spell the end of a relationship.

"Such as?"

"Well..." Julie scanned the light over the pages again. "Maybe she's writing a romance novel."

"That's sure stretching things."

"You said yourself that she took some creative writing electives in college. Suppose she decided to turn her writing to novels? Listen to this and tell me if it sounds romancy to you.''

She cleared her throat and began speaking in a low, whispery voice, as if to lend an aura of silk sheets and roses to her recitation. "'As he leaned toward me, his warm breath lightly brushed my cheek. Though we'd only met a few hours ago, I couldn't wait for him to kiss me. So when his left hand ventured to my waist and his right thigh brushed mine, I tipped my head back and waited for his lips to brush my eager mouth.'''

Against his will, Hunter conjured up the image of a certain dark-haired, freckle-faced young woman tipping her face in invitation to him, and his body responded as if the picture in his mind was real. To distract himself from the path his thoughts were leading him, he interrupted Julie's reading.

"If it's an attempt at fiction, it'll never sell," he declared. "There are too many repeated words—namely, *brushed* and *brush*. It reads like an instruction manual, and most novels use 'she' and 'her' instead of 'I' and 'me.'"

Julie flashed him a devious smile. "You seem to know the genre very well. Are romances your preferred bedtime reading?"

Why did she have to mention bedtime? His body was already on hyperalert.

"And she doesn't use the guy's name," he said, ignoring her taunt, "which leads me to believe it's a real person."

As if she hadn't heard his comment, Julie turned her attention back to the file. "This doesn't make sense. 'Then he proceeded to nudge my right foot with his, brushing the sandal that dangled there until he had knocked it off, denuding my foot.'"

"Remind me to give her a thesaurus for Christmas."

"And a mail-order writing course while you're at it. How can he be brushing her thigh with his leg while at the same time he's 'denuding' her right foot?"

Julie's lips puckered in puzzlement, and Hunter wanted nothing more than to "brush" his mouth against them, as Anna had described in her writings. "They had to have been sitting, probably with him on the left and her on the right, like we are now."

She peered at him and then again at the papers. "Okay, now I think I get it. Maybe the music was loud and he leaned close to be heard when he spoke to her.''

With her gaze still glued to the file, she reached across and drew Hunter's left hand toward her waist. He happily obliged, leaning toward her and inhaling the fresh, tangy scent of her perfume. The gearshift dug into his knee, and he scooted past it so his thigh touched hers as described in Anna's essay. In the quiet of the night, their breathing echoed loudly in the car.

Reacting to his closeness, Julie mimicked Anna's reaction by tilting her face upward. Her lips parted slightly, forming a soft O. Without a will of his own, Hunter leaned toward her to complete the scene that had been set up in the poorly written pages. Then, remembering something, he stopped.

"You have to cross your right leg over your left."

Julie blinked twice, as if bringing herself back from a faraway place, and did as she was told. Now she seemed self-consciously aware of their closeness.

Her innocent reaction to this bit of playacting turned him on more than if she had wantonly come on to him. He wanted her—now!—but he purposely prolonged initiating the kiss that both of them craved. She dropped her gaze, and her long lashes fluttered nervously over her freckled cheeks.

Lifting his sneakered foot, he teased her backless shoe until it dropped with a small thud. As if anticipating the next part, Julie gave him a shy grin.

"Oops," he said, his voice erupting in a husky croak. "I 'denuded' you."

One corner of her mouth lifted, and Hunter yearned to explore the gentle curve of it with his own. His hand slid upward until his thumb grazed the curve of her breast. Julie drew in a breath at his touch, and Hunter urged her closer until they were a hairsbreadth from the kiss that waited tauntingly for them.

Sliding his free hand behind her neck and feeling the weight of her thick hair in his fingers, he drew Julie closer until their lips touched—light, warm and tingling with desire and anticipation.

By now, Hunter's breath was coming more quickly, and he wished he'd bought a van rather than an SUV. Her skin was soft, like the new chamois cloths he'd bought to wax the car. Julie's lips acquiesced under his gentle exploration. She reached for him, clutching his shirt with eager fingers. His body responded in a way that turned out to be painful in the tight confines of the car's bucket seat.

Hunter shifted position, trying to ease the discomfort that grew more unbearable with each second that passed. He wanted to be lying down with her under him. Even better, with himself inside her as he drank in the sweetness of her kiss....

A flash of light at the corner of his eye drew his attention back to the house. Reluctant to disturb the teasing give and take of tongue on tongue, he tried to ignore the subtle signal to return to work. A second later, when it registered on his kiss-drugged brain that activity in the house had changed, he abruptly ended the exchange that had, for a long moment, made him forget all about why he was here tonight.

"Damn, they're gone!"

Julie looked stunned by his sudden change in attitude. "We could buy some more at the drugstore down the street."

It took him a moment to understand what she was saying, and he wished like hell they could do exactly as she suggested.

"I'm talking about Anna," he explained. "A light is on at the other end of the house. Probably a bedroom."

He pushed open the vehicle door while Julie registered what he'd said. With still camera in hand—the videocam was beyond use after Mrs. Ramsey's attack on it—he eased the car door closed behind him without letting it click. Julie followed him across the lawn to the house. He waved her back so she wouldn't accidentally call attention to them, but as usual, she ignored him. Hunter just sighed and lifted the latch on the wooden gate to let himself into the side yard. Julie waited a short distance away.

Pressing against the spindly, overgrown bushes near the house, he lifted his camera, hoping what he found would be completely innocent, but knowing that wasn't very likely, given Anna's secretiveness. It was difficult to see between the slats of the nearly closed blinds but, to his disappointment, he was able to make out his sister-in-law lying on a poster bed with a lacy comforter rumpled seductively around her. Wearing a pink lace teddy, she struck an alluring pose on the bed, and Hunter felt his stomach reel. A movement to one side indicated someone had just left the room, but he didn't catch the identity of that person.

"What do you see?" Julie whispered from her post on the other side of the fence.

Hunter waved again, this time to hush her.

Setting the camera's F-stops so that he wouldn't need the flash, he squeezed the shutter to capture the damning shot. A tiny click confirmed that the image had been committed to film. The camera would automatically add evidence with the date and time stamp in the lower-right corner of the shot.

The bedroom door opened, and a hand appeared, gripping the edge. Hunter shifted his position to aim through the slats, and poised his camera for the next bit of unwelcome news in the unfolding of Anna's secret life.

"Hunter."

He couldn't believe Julie was being so naive as to call out his name. Another second and he'd see the body and face that belonged to the hand on the door.

"*Hunter.*" Though she was whispering, the intensity was enough to get his—and possibly their subjects'—attention.

He whirled toward the fence, determined never to ask Julie to accompany him on a stakeout again, no matter how delicious her kisses were.

Her eyes were wide with fear, and she was pointing at something behind him.

"Dog!"

A snarl reached his ears as he felt the presence of the beast lunging toward him.

Hunter dropped the camera and ran for his life.

The sideboard drawer opened with ease, revealing a blank pad of paper, a pencil, two dried-up pens and a bent paper clip. Julie reached behind the junk and closed her fingers around a small book. The journal, covered with red-ink stamp marks of puckered lips, felt heavier than usual in her hands, mimicking the way this assignment was weighing on her mind. She pushed the drawer shut.

The page fell open to the latest entry, and she wondered if it was cheating to list Hunter multiple times. The number scores showed that, while he had started at the top of the chart, he had still managed to improve with each subsequent kiss.

But no matter how high he rated in her personal ranking, Julie knew she needed to get more kisses to compare against his. She still didn't trust her judgment when it came to men. Not after the way she'd fallen for a man in college who turned out to be totally unsuited to her. Geoff had been as pretentious as the spelling of his name, but she hadn't seen it until he'd dumped her for refusing to sleep with him. She hadn't noticed how shallow he was until he immediately took up with a member of the girls' volleyball team, a buxom babe who wore no bra and very little fabric that passed for a shirt.

Julie wasn't going to make that mistake again. And she believed wholeheartedly that the only way to avoid similar mistakes was to follow Gran's advice and kiss the required one hundred men for comparison and contrast. Julie sighed. She truly believed a man's personality was revealed in his kiss, and she knew this was a way for her to learn more about the male of her species. Too bad she wanted to stop with number forty-seven. She thought back to last night in Hunter's SUV, and a distinct feeling of warmth swept over her.

The doorbell rang, and Julie started at the sound. Clutching the small book to her chest, she crossed the room and squinted out the door's peephole.

It was Hunter. And he had something in his hands. It was too big to be a bill for his broken and lost cameras and shredded pants.

She turned and debated for a second where to stash the book. He'd certainly hear the drawer if she pulled it open to return it to its previous hiding place, and she was sure he'd be brazen enough to ask what she was hiding from him.

"Just a minute," she called, hoping to stall for another second or two.

Her gaze fell on the magazine rack beside the recliner, and she shoved it in there, smugly certain that an item in plain sight would not attract notice.

When she opened the door, Hunter's handsome eyes were shadowed.

"What's the matter?" she asked, beckoning him inside. If she didn't know him better, she might have thought he was angry with her. But that wasn't it. Something else was troubling him.

He merely shook his head and stood in her living room as if deciding what to do or say next.

"Would you like a beer? I also have iced tea and cherry Kool-Aid."

He flashed her a quick smile. "Tea would be nice."

When she came back with two drinks, he had already made himself comfortable on the couch. She handed him one of the glasses and put the other on the coffee table.

He held it up to the lamplight and examined the reddish-brown liquid. "This is tea?"

"Iced tea and cherry Kool-Aid," she said, taking a seat beside him. "It's very good."

"I should have known. After all, you didn't say tea *or* Kool-Aid."

He took a sip, then passed his tongue over his lips as if savoring the taste. That simple gesture had Julie's imagination conjuring up a scenario featuring the sweet red drink, joined lips and very few clothes.

"Not bad."

Indeed.

"I'm really sorry about last night." Julie drank some tea, hoping the cold liquid would quell her errant thoughts. "If I'd known that brute was going to be so vicious, I would have—"

"There wasn't anything else you could have done. Don't worry about it."

"Your pants were completely shredded."

"I can buy more." He straightened and turned toward her as if signaling that it was time to move on to another topic.

"But what about the gash on your ankle? Maybe you should get a tetanus shot. That nail head on the gate might have been rusty."

"The cut is going to be fine, and all my shots are up-to-date."

Julie relaxed at that bit of good news. "It's a wonder that dog didn't bite more than your pants. I've heard papillons can be territorial, but I never knew they could run so fast."

"Papillon? I thought it was a hairy Chihuahua with big fuzzy bat wings for ears."

Although they laughed at the memory of what had happened last night, Julie had worried at the time that the little beast would take a chunk out of Hunter.

She waited, knowing that Hunter's efficiency would not allow him to dawdle long before getting to the point of his visit.

He handed her a small package wrapped in navy paper and clumsily tied with a thin red ribbon. She gazed up at him, wondering what had prompted him to do something so unexpected, but he just nodded toward the package.

She slid the ribbon off and removed the paper without tearing it. Inside was a small, pink, flower-covered datebook with separate sections for keeping track of appointments, to-do lists and phone calls.

Puzzled by this unexpected gift, she lifted her gaze to him for an explanation.

"My secretary will be coming back to work soon." He fidgeted with the bit of ribbon that had fallen onto the plaid sofa cushion. "The book should be helpful in landing and keeping a job." Reacting to her lifted eyebrow, he added gently, "So you won't forget to do things."

Julie lifted her chin. "I don't forget...I just get busy with other things."

He grinned at her defensive response, and Julie realized she'd sounded ungracious. "Thank you," she said. "I appreciate the thought."

And she did. Time management and attention to details were important to him, and he wanted to share this part of himself with her. She knew her cluttered desk and haphazard approach to tasks drove him crazy and tested his patience. Although she would never be driven by clocks and schedules the way Hunter was, she conceded it wouldn't hurt to learn to use the day planner. After all, once she was hired as a reporter, she'd have to juggle lots of details and running from interview to interview. Hunter's gift might help make that part of her job a little easier.

Leaning toward him, she kissed his cheek. "This was very sweet of you. I'll put it to good use."

He accepted the kiss mindlessly, his thoughts clearly elsewhere. Julie's disappointment that her action didn't prompt a return kiss was overshadowed by the knowledge that the gift was not the primary reason he had come here tonight.

A moment of silence hung between them before he spilled what was on his mind. "I'm going to have to tell Peter about Anna."

"That she's the mystery kisser?" Julie's stomach clenched at the thought of someone else being unjustly blamed for something she had done. "That writing sample we read last night—" And acted out, she remembered wistfully. "—didn't sound anything like the columnist's style."

"It was probably a rough first draft. And the editor probably cleans it up some more. But that's not what I was talking about. I'm going to have to tell him that his wife is cheating on him." Hunter slouched back against the couch and put a hand to his forehead. "Gosh, I wish I could unsee what I saw last night."

"You don't really know what you saw," Julie reminded him. "You have no idea who that other person was, and there could be a simple explanation for Anna's being there. Who knows, she could have been doing a dress rehearsal for a play, and maybe she's planning to surprise everyone with her performance on opening night."

Without lifting his head, Hunter slanted her a skeptical glance. "I feel guilty for having followed Anna—a woman I love like a sister—and even worse for what I have to report to Peter." He took a deep breath and stared at the ceiling. "There's nothing in the procedure manual that tells how to handle something like this."

Julie scooted closer and took his hand in hers. A

bandage graced the knuckle of his pinky finger, which he'd slammed in the gate last night. She'd never realized until then that he possessed such a broad vocabulary of four-letter words.

He looked at her and pulled her to him, draping one arm around her shoulders.

"You don't have to tell him, you know." Julie's fingers rested on his chest, and she played idly with the buttons of his shirt. "You could just take yourself off the case, maybe have a private chat with Anna and convince her to tell her husband what's going on."

Hunter covered her hand with his, dwarfing it in comparison. "Anna has gone to great lengths to hide what she's doing from him, so it's not likely she'll change her mind. If I'm less than a hundred percent honest with Peter, then I'll be every bit as deceptive as she has been." He sighed, as if releasing a great weight he'd been carrying.

"I can't tolerate dishonesty in myself," he added, "any more than I can tolerate it in others."

Julie looked away from him, her gaze falling on her notebook, covered with red lip prints. It seemed to taunt her with all forty-seven of its secrets.

Chapter Seven

It's amazing what a kiss can reveal about a person. The first one tells about his personality and mood. But the more you kiss a man, the more you learn about his quirks and even his sense of integrity.

Julie jerked her eyes back to Hunter, hoping he hadn't noticed what she'd been staring at. He met her gaze, and her insides turned to mush. She set the day planner on the coffee table and kicked off her sneakers. "For someone who's such a stickler for schedules and to-do lists," she said, loosening the top button of her shirt in invitation, "it's hard to believe you've left one major project unfinished."

They wanted each other. She knew it. But circumstance, and perhaps Hunter's overdeveloped sense of responsibility, had kept them from following through on the feelings that flowed between them. Tonight, however, she would make it clear that she was a grown woman who knew what she wanted.

And what she wanted was Hunter.

His heavy-lidded stare told her he knew exactly what unfinished business she was talking about. He dragged a thumb over the scar at the corner of his mouth, and Julie knew that tonight there would be no surveillance subjects to interrupt them.

To her relief and delight, Hunter grasped her behind the knees and stretched her denim-clad legs across his lap. Then, going from the opposite direction, he opened the bottom button of her shirt, which barely skimmed her waistline. The action laid bare a winter-pale glimpse of navel adorned by a clear blue bead on a tiny silver hoop.

Julie had never been so frustrated as last night, when the surveillance subject's bedroom activity had prevented their own. Tonight, however, would be different. Provided, of course, she could keep her eyes and thoughts off that blasted lips-covered notebook.

Hunter's strong fingers massaged the dip of her waist. As he leaned ever closer, she could feel his desire where he pressed against the back of her thigh, and the knowledge that he wanted her in this way fueled her own rapturous yearnings.

She leaned back against the plush cushions, and twin hundred-watt glares beat down on them from the reading lamps at each end of the couch. But what seemed to shine the brightest was her kissing notebook, which looked as though it might topple from its precarious place among the magazines.

With effort, she pulled herself upright and rose to her bare feet. As she did so, Hunter's hands slid from her waist to her hips and then down to her thighs.

"Where are you going?" he asked, stroking her knee. "I'm prepared."

Julie bent and kissed him, taking note of the gentle yet urgent pressure of his lips on hers. "I need to take care of something."

Namely, moving the book to a better hiding place, but she'd let him think it was to dim the lights. When she moved across the room toward the first lamp, he apparently misunderstood, thinking she was calling a halt to their lovemaking.

"While you're doing that," he said, rising from the couch, "I'll give Peter a call. This situation with Anna is going to bug me until I do the right thing."

Julie gulped and switched off the first light as he made his way to the phone in the kitchen. He was right. He was an honest man, and something like this would nag at his conscience until everything was out in the open. She picked up the book and considered what he was doing. Hunter knew it would hurt his brother, and himself as well, when he revealed what they had discovered last night. But his dread of an unpleasant confrontation was not keeping him from doing the right thing.

She flicked off the other lamp and sat back down on the couch, the scorebook resting on her lap. After she told him the truth, it was doubtful they'd need the lights dimmed for romance. But at least she could take refuge in the comfort of the shadows while she told him her secret. And the low lighting would prevent her from seeing just how badly she had hurt the man she'd loved all her life.

She did love him. At first it had been with the little-girl admiration of someone who had taken on superhero traits in her mind. Later, it had been with an immense crush of hero-worship proportions. And now, as an adult, it was with the maturity of a woman with a grown-up understanding of the true meaning of forever...and honesty and putting the other before yourself.

She would have to trust him. Trust him to keep her secret, sure, but more than that, trust him to understand why she'd made the choices she had. To understand why she hadn't told him before when there had been so many opportunities to do so.

When he returned, he took off his suit jacket and draped it over the arm of the couch before sitting beside her. "Very romantic," he said, taking her in his arms once again. "Want to pick up where we left off?"

She couldn't bring herself to look him in the eye. But instead of launching into the discussion she'd planned, she sidestepped the issue with a question of her own. "Did you get in touch with your brother?"

He nuzzled her neck. "Yeah, I called him, but he'd had a bad day at work. It seemed cruel to kick him while he's down, so I just told him the truth—that we didn't know anything definitive yet."

She straightened, and the kissing notebook almost fell off her lap. Grateful for the room's concealing darkness, she grabbed for the book, wondering how—or if—she was going to tell Hunter her secret. "You didn't tell him?"

He nipped her ear and slid an arm around her waist, saying in no uncertain terms that he didn't want to waste energy talking when there were better things for them to do. She couldn't agree more. But that still didn't solve her dilemma.

"No, I'm going to give it time," he murmured

into her ear. "This is one of those occasions when it's best to wait on delivering hurtful information."

Julie felt her head loll under his loving ministrations, and once again she lay back against the cushions. With the cloud of passion blurring her thoughts, it would be impossible to concentrate on what she needed to tell him. In his pain for his brother's heartache, Hunter was every bit as vulnerable as Peter. Just as Hunter had spared delivering bad news at a bad time, perhaps she should do the same for him.

Dropping her hand to the floor, she tucked the book under the couch. Hunter hovered over her, his biceps bunching under his white dress shirt as he dropped teasing kisses on her lips. Yes, she agreed silently, sometimes it was best to wait on giving someone hurtful information. And this, thank heavens, was one of those times.

She loosened the knot of his tie and, tugging on both ends, urged him ever closer until his full weight rested on her. It felt good to be lying so intimately with him. His forearms cradled her head, and he played with her ponytail clasp until it released a cascade of brown waves. Suddenly aware of how frumpy she must look, she wished she hadn't changed into casual clothes after she got home from work.

"I must look a sight," she said, reaching to smooth her rumpled hair.

Arching his back, Hunter fumbled with his belt, then unfastened her jeans and slid her zipper down with excruciating calm. "A beautiful sight," he amended. "Here you are in jeans, bare feet and falling-down ponytail, yet you turn me on more than any supermodel ever could."

He helped tug the jeans off her hips and flung them to the floor, followed by his slacks.

"That's what I love about you," he said, his voice so low it vibrated against her skin. "There's no pretense."

Once he'd opened her shirt and relieved her of her bra, Hunter took the silk tie from her trembling hands and dragged it over her bare breasts. He followed its path with a trail of kisses, and Julie almost cried out from sheer ecstasy.

Drawing his hands from her shoulders to the taut, tender swells, he stroked her the way a potter might caress a beautiful, curved vase. "Look at you," he said. "You're the most WYSIWYG person I know."

The unusual word stilled the exploration of Julie's fingers over the broad expanse of his back. Though she'd heard the term before, she couldn't recall exactly what it meant. "WYSIWYG?"

He touched his tongue to the hollow beneath her neck. "Mmm. What you see is what you get. And, boy, do I like what I'm seeing."

Julie wriggled under him. A conscience was a good thing to have...except maybe at times like this.

He mistook her movement for encouragement and slid an arm under her back, then dipped an exploring finger beneath the waistband of her panties.

"I can't...." Julie struggled to rise, but she was trapped beneath him—a heavenly prison. "We can't do this."

"We can't, or shouldn't?" Hunter peered at her through the meager light that spilled into the room from the kitchen.

"Both."

His confusion was evident as he moved aside, and

she was aware of him watching her hurriedly gather their clothes together.

"It just wouldn't be right," she said.

It was a terrible thing to do, changing course without so much as a hint of warning. But Julie knew without a doubt that if their lovemaking proceeded any further, such an intimate betrayal would be even more unforgivable than the deception she had already inflicted on him.

"It wouldn't be right at all."

If there was anything Julie had learned about Hunter last night, it was that he was a true gentleman. Any other man might have been infuriated by her sudden change of heart, but Hunter had accepted her decision without pressuring her to continue. True, he'd looked confused and even hurt, but he had respected her choice, even though she could not give him a reasonable explanation for it.

Julie reached across the desk and shook the hand of the woman who had just introduced herself as Hunter's secretary.

"I'm Julie Fasano, your fill-in. Are you back to work already?"

"Goodness, no," Trudy said with a friendly laugh. "I'm just here to pick up my paycheck."

Julie reached into the cash box and pulled out a pay envelope marked with Trudy's name. "It's wonderful to finally meet you," she told the woman standing before her. "I've heard a lot of wonderful things about you."

If Trudy was anything at all the way she appeared, then she was every bit as exacting as everyone claimed her to be. Hunter's secretary wasn't the most beautiful woman Julie had ever seen, but she certainly was the most perfect. Although her blond hair had been tucked up with an alligator clip, every hair lay in rigid order and the casual "do" looked as formal as a teased and sprayed chignon. Her white shirt and starched tan pants were complemented by a silver-buckled black belt, and her running shoes appeared as crisp and clean as those worn by a nurse. Even her fingernails were perfectly filed to a squared-off tip and polished with a smooth white French trim.

By comparison, Julie felt incredibly inadequate. She casually straightened one of the many piles on her—no, Trudy's—desk and tossed a couple of scraps of paper she'd used as doodle sheets into the trash can. It made no appreciable difference.

"It's good to meet you, too. Everybody in the office is just crazy about you, and I have to admit to a certain amount of curiosity." Trudy tucked her pay envelope into a zippered pocket inside her leather purse and leaned toward Julie as if to share a secret. "None of their descriptions do you justice," she said with a warm, open smile.

That simple gesture dissolved all of Julie's uncertainties about meeting the other woman, who meant so much to Hunter. "He's not in right now," she said, waving toward his office.

Eager to get on with her new career, Julie had been subconsciously counting the days until her trial period with the newspaper would be over. But now that Hunter's secretary was standing in front of her, that time felt too close...too real.

"No problem," said Trudy, unconcerned. "That'll give us a chance to talk. Since I'm here, is there anything you'd like to ask about the duties Hunter is giving you?"

"I'm glad you asked." Julie rose to her feet, belatedly remembering to gather her shoes and slide them back on. "There are so many details to keep track of with all this paperwork that it's hard to keep up. Do you have any tips for preventing things from falling through the cracks?"

The least she could do, after letting Hunter down last night, was not let him down at the office. Even more than disappointing him by pulling back at such an intimate time, she regretted misleading him into thinking of her as an unpretentious "WYSIWYG" person when, in fact, she'd been deceiving him all along.

"The best thing you can do is get yourself a good planner." Trudy dug into her purse and handed a small binder to Julie to peruse. "I wouldn't be caught dead without mine."

Julie flipped through the carefully annotated pages and smiled. "No wonder you and Hunter get along so well. You're both perfectionists."

The other woman's lips pressed into a thin line. Julie returned the book, and Trudy returned it to the exact spot she had taken it from in her purse. "Give yourself time. You'll learn Hunter's quirks and get used to them after a while."

Julie shrugged. She wouldn't be here long enough for that to happen, but she couldn't help wanting to learn more about his personal quirks—like what he ate for breakfast, and how he felt about foreign movies. "You look rested," she told Trudy. "You must be enjoying your honeymoon."

Trudy smiled, and her perfectly accentuated lips

spread upward in a symmetrical bow. ''I wish it would never end. First we went to the Bahamas for some time in the sun—''

Julie couldn't help noticing that the new bride was barely tanned at all—the sign of a successful honeymoon.

''—and now we're busy painting and decorating our new house.'' She shifted her purse to the other shoulder and gave Julie a conspiratorial smile. ''Mark and I are thinking about making some other changes as well.''

Was it Julie's imagination, or did Trudy surreptitiously touch a hand to her abdomen? Against her will, Julie felt a surge of envy spread through her at the thought of yet another peer achieving her own goal of marriage and family before her. Not that she begrudged Trudy the happiness that she herself sought but, doggone it, Julie wanted it, too. A handsome husband—or at the very least, one who could kiss with integrity—and a baby or two. Or three. Maybe even four. Whatever the number, she wanted to get started soon. But that wasn't bound to happen until she kissed fifty-three more men and knew for certain that the man she would marry was truly her perfect match.

Those well-laid plans, unfortunately, had been thwarted by Hunter's kisses. For now the thought of kissing even one or two more men held all the appeal of, well, endless paperwork at a deskbound job.

''It sounds like married life is agreeing with you.'' Julie slouched and tucked a stray tendril behind her ear. She wondered if Trudy had kissed a hundred men before committing herself to the man who was now her husband.

"More than I ever imagined." Trudy lowered herself into the guest chair in front of the desk. "Mark is a wonderful man. He's funny and sweet. And he has this way of taking charge of things that is neither intimidating nor controlling... It's a pleasure to be with him when we work on our many projects together."

Julie could think of one project she would have enjoyed working on with Hunter. She sighed. "He sounds a lot like Hunter."

Trudy squared her shoulders and clenched her purse with both hands. Julie was amused to note that her lone bit of disarray was a single thread of yellow yarn that dangled from beneath the purse flap. Baby booties, perhaps?

"No, he's nothing like Hunter." Though Trudy's tone was calm, she seemed disturbed by the comparison. "Mark is easygoing...mellow, even."

"You'd be surprised," Julie said, rising to their mutual employer's defense. "Hunter can let his hair down at times." Not often, but the potential was there.

She received an assessing stare in response, and realized she may have said too much. Before Trudy could follow up on the indiscretion, Julie diverted the conversation back to a previous topic.

"This change that you and Mark are considering... What's holding you back?"

The woman hesitated a long moment, obviously weighing her response. "It will most likely inconvenience other people. It's reasonable to expect they might not be happy with our decision."

Was Trudy referring to in-laws who thought it was too soon to start a family? Or was she concerned about Hunter being inconvenienced while she was out on maternity leave? Whatever the case, outsiders had no place in such a personal decision.

"It sounds like you're torn between doing what others want and doing what you and Mark want."

"Torn? How about ripped apart?" Trudy stood and, for the first time, seemed awkward in her movements. "I want to do the right thing and not let people down, but my heart is calling me to make this big change in my life."

Julie stepped forward and touched her arm in a show of sisterly support. "You need to do what's right for *you*...what's right for you and Mark. You'll never go wrong if you follow your heart."

Her own words sounded like déjà vu, and then she remembered that Ethel had written something very similar in her final column. Was Julie now dispensing the very advice that she had once argued against? She tipped her head to one side. Well, in this particular case, it was what Hunter's secretary needed to hear.

Trudy met her gaze, and an expression of peace fell over her polished features. "Thank you," she said, relaxing the death grip on her purse. "You've helped me more than you can imagine."

"I'm glad to be of service." Julie gathered up her purse and programmed the phone to ring on Priscilla's desk. "Why don't I buy you lunch, and you can repay me by sharing all the paperwork shortcuts you know?"

Good grief, now she'd made front-page news. Front page of the *Flair* section, that is.

Julie flipped the paper over and read the headline again: Who Is the Mystery Kisser?

In a poorly concealed attempt to avoid journalism's incestuous no-no of writing about one of its own, her editor had assigned a reporter to cover the radio station's contest and listeners' reactions to the "Uncommon Wisdom" column. She supposed she should be grateful that her column had stirred so much curiosity among readers, and that the paper was taking advantage of the publicity, but how was she supposed to remain anonymous if even her own editor seemed to be conspiring against her?

Since her hopes for continuing the column rode on keeping Ann Onimus in the shadows, she considered calling Mr. Upshaw to suggest he not call any further attention to her true identity. But a paranoid fear that either of their telephones might be tapped prompted her to forgo that course of action.

Hunter appeared at her desk, looking as upset as she felt. He'd been acting very businesslike with her lately—ever since that night at her house, when they'd almost made love—and now he seemed even more tense than usual. Not that she blamed him. She'd been tense herself, a condition that would have been relieved if only her conscience had allowed her to finish what they had started.

When he was like this, she could understand why Trudy had disagreed so sharply about him sharing similar qualities with her husband. *Easygoing* was not exactly the word Julie would use to describe him right now.

The sound of the radio drifted from his office, reminding Julie that in her shock over this morning's headline, she'd forgotten to tune in to the *Burning Issues* show.

"The radio station's sponsors have added to the prize for the person who finds the mystery kisser." The grip-exerciser squeaked repeatedly in Hunter's hand. "The cosmetics store is offering a year's supply of lipstick. A dentist will give away a bleaching kit. And a drugstore is giving free breath mints to anyone who brings in a copy of the mystery kisser's column."

Not knowing how to respond, Julie pushed the jar of toffees toward him. Gran had always given her a piece of candy when she was upset. Hunter seemed not to notice the gesture, so she took one for herself.

He shifted the exerciser to the other hand and began anew. "I want you to write a memo for my signature and distribute it to everyone on staff. Tell them I will match those prizes and kick in a bonus of one thousand dollars to anyone who finds the mystery kisser before the radio station finds out."

The toffee stuck in her throat and triggered a coughing spasm. Hunter stepped closer and patted her back. The scent of his cologne had the intoxicating effect of soothing her as it brought forth memories of him lying with her on the couch, sharing kisses and tender touches. When her coughing eased, she was disappointed when he removed his hand from her back, once again putting a coldly proper distance between them.

Pulling a pad of paper from under two blended stacks of files, she wondered what it would have been like if she had met Hunter again under other circumstances. Circumstances that did not involve secrets and white lies.

Hunter was a man of honor. His strongly honed sense of integrity, while amended slightly for surveillance purposes, would not allow him to be less than fully honest and forthright in his personal dealings. And, understandably so, he would expect no less from the woman who would eventually share his life…and his bed.

Julie sighed and scribbled down what he wanted her to say in the memo. The public curiosity inspired by her column could—depending on how events unfolded—assure her a full-time reporting job or convince the editor that she was unable to keep a low profile.

The situation had escalated with the radio sponsors' response and, as a consequence, her need to remain anonymous had increased as well. Just a few more days, she told herself as she bit her cheek to keep from blurting out the truth. Just a few more days.

"Emphasize in the memo that the terms require they find the mystery kisser before the radio gets wind of it." He tucked the gripper in his hip pocket. "And, of course, there must be complete secrecy. No one—not at the radio station, or even here at Oltmeier-Matthews—must know about the mystery kisser's identity other than myself."

Secrecy for *him*, maybe, but there would be no secrecy for her. Bending over the pad, she avoided eye contact by focusing on her notes.

"I'm hoping it won't be Anna," he conceded, "in which case we'll release the information to the radio station and enjoy the free publicity."

Julie gulped, then reflexively put a hand to her throat.

"But, on the off chance it *is* Anna, it would be better if everyone doesn't know it right away. Even as little as a few hours might buy us enough time to devise an appropriate plan of action before her name is made public."

Before *Julie's* name was made public, was her silent amendment. A few more days of stiff formality and guarded looks, she reminded herself. And then they'd both be free to move on with their lives.

Their separate lives.

Chapter Eight

In matters of kissing, as well as in other areas of life, one may find oneself pondering the dilemma of when and whether it's appropriate to tell the truth. Bad breath, for instance. Should you come right out and tell him, or stay quiet and assume he'll figure it out for himself?

The credit check on Anna looked, at first glance, to be that of a woman who could be trusted. The card issued solely in her name showed a pattern of being paid off in full every month. But a closer examination of the charges applied over the past few weeks showed a less-than-respectable side of the woman they'd been following.

Any one of the purchases by itself would not have raised an eyebrow, but put them all together and the items revealed a sad, but telling, story. Expensive lingerie. Fine restaurants. A photographer's studio, which Julie assumed meant that Anna may have had sweetheart photos made. And even a hotel bill for the romantic landmark building that was rumored to have been the setting of the famous staircase scene in *Gone with the Wind*.

Julie was worried for Anna. And more than a little uneasy about her own role in having Anna watched. Sure, the woman's activity probably would have raised suspicion in her husband's mind anyway, but it was Julie's column that had prompted Peter to solicit Hunter's help. Worried that her activities, if taken to a public forum, might harm his judicial career in addition to his marriage, Peter had turned to his younger brother for answers.

Sighing, Julie set the sheet facedown on Hunter's stack and picked up the next one. The tidbits of advice Trudy had offered over lunch were of little help in getting control of the clutter on her desk. The sheer volume of mostly useless data was enough to make Julie grind her teeth in frustration. How did perfectionists like Hunter and Trudy manage to keep up with so much...well, Julie was too much of a lady to even think the word.

She considered shoving all the little piles into one big one and setting a match to it, but that wouldn't take care of the problem with Anna. Picking up the next credit report in that same batch, Julie found her attention immediately drawn to the subject's name: Juliet Elizabeth Fasano. The social security number matched her own, so this was not a case of a client who happened to have the same name.

Turning her chair so that she could see Hunter if he should come out of his office, she scanned the report. Although it showed a top-notch rating, she wasn't quite as good as Anna about reducing her balance to zero every statement. But at the rate she was going, the living-room set would be paid off in another couple of months.

But why had this information come to Hunter? Had he been tipped off? Was he investigating her as well as his sister-in-law?

Julie flipped to the next section of the report. In addition to her purchase and payment history, the digital printout also listed everyone who had accessed her information recently. Credit-card companies, the furniture company prior to approving her loan, and…Regalia Communications Corporation.

A vein throbbed in her temple. RCC was the parent company of the *Richmond Reporter*. She vaguely remembered signing a blanket employment agreement allowing them to conduct a background investigation, and had probably done the same thing when she was hired at Oltmeier-Matthews—it was hard to remember. Since she'd had nothing to hide, she hadn't thought twice about what her employers might be looking into. Or that one might be made aware of the other's search.

Folding the papers with the print toward the inside and laying the incriminating evidence on her desk, Julie pondered her next course of action.

One, she could file the report in her personnel folder and hope he never noticed it. But a bloodhound was more likely to overlook a fresh steak.

Two, she could ''lose'' the document—a believable scenario, given the condition of her desk—and pretend it had never existed. Knowing Hunter, however, he probably had it noted in that blasted calendar of his when to expect the report. If it mysteriously disappeared, he'd probably just order another copy, but that could buy her enough time to finish out her gig here until Trudy returned and Julie was hired permanently as a newspaper columnist and reporter.

Or three, she could just hand it over to him. And prepare for flying fetid material to hit the fan.

Gee, and she had thought choosing between the country-blue couch and the plaid one had been a hard decision. Julie bit at the corner of her fingernail, wishing Gran had taught her a wise proverb for a situation such as this. All she could think of was if she told a lie her nose would grow. If that were true, it should be ten feet long by now.

Taking a deep breath to steady her nerves, Julie gathered up the papers out of the box marked Hunter. Then, almost as an afterthought, she tucked her credit report in her slacks pocket.

Hunter hung up the phone as Julie entered his office. He wondered if she'd been sleeping lately. She usually wore a sunny smile, even when griping about having to handle too many details at once, but today she wore a weary expression. The mood matched his own.

"That was Peter on the phone. He knows."

Julie looked surprised. "He does? And he told you?"

Hunter leaned back in his chair and rubbed the back of his neck. "What are you talking about? I told him everything we learned about Anna."

"Oh." She lowered her head and stared at the carpet, almost as if she were the guilty one. She reached one hand into her pocket and crinkled a paper before taking the chair beside his desk. "There's more," she said. "And it doesn't look good. None of it."

He took the paper she handed him and studied the details about Anna's credit transactions as Julie set the rest of the stack in his In box. No, indeed, it didn't look good. "It doesn't matter," he said, as much to himself as to Julie. "Peter has already decided to ask for a divorce."

"Oh, no!" She clutched a hand to her heart. "I feel so bad about all of this."

"There's no need for you to take it personally. She brought it on herself." Even to his own ears, his comment sounded cold and unfeeling. Julie's startled reaction confirmed that she thought so, too. "There are lines," he said. "Lines in a relationship that should never be crossed. And trust and honesty are right up there at the top."

Julie nervously touched a hand to her pocket again. "But Anna's not—"

"Save your breath." Hunter would not give her the opportunity to defend Anna. "Convincing me of her innocence will accomplish nothing, since it's Peter's decision to make. And if it were mine, I'd be doing the same thing."

"But if you'd let me explain—"

"No, let *me* explain." Hunter felt literally sick to his stomach. This whole episode had brought the pain of his own ill-fated engagement back as if it were a present-day reality. Although he and Julie had been tense with each other lately and he couldn't figure out why she had pulled away from him—away from a closeness such as he had never shared with anyone else, not even his former fiancée—he couldn't help opening up to her now. He leaned for-

ward and covered her hand with his own, willing her
to listen. "A couple of years ago, something happened that made me understand how important it is
not to withhold things from people who are close to
you."

Releasing her hand, he stood and paced the floor.
"I was engaged to be married...to someone I thought
I could trust. It was a Saturday night, and we were
planning to attend a musical Yvonne had been waiting for months to see. While I was in my room
changing my tie, the phone rang and she picked it
up."

He glanced over at Julie, who was riffling the cor-
ners of the papers she'd brought. She seemed sad,
and he wanted to hold her, but even more, he wanted
her to know why he supported his brother's difficult
decision. That he wasn't being judgmental or unkind.

"It was Len, my partner, who called. He asked her
to tell me that he needed my assistance." Hunter
paused and straightened the wall graph depicting the
number of cases solved since he'd joined the firm.
With each succeeding month, the line had moved
steadily upward. "She assumed that he wanted me
to help him on a case, which would mean missing
the show, so she decided to wait until the curtain
dropped before giving me the message. As it turned
out, Len was having chest pains and wanted me to
take him to the hospital, but he didn't want to worry
me by coming right out and saying so."

Julie cleared her throat. "Was it a heart attack?"

"No, it turned out to be gallstones, which was
serious enough in itself. But it could have been much
worse." He hated to consider the possibility. Len
was his mentor and friend, and Hunter couldn't bear

to think of the devastating turn that night might have taken.

"She didn't know, Hunter." Julie's tone was soft, and she seemed to be asking him to find forgiveness in his heart. But that was something he was not prepared to do.

"If a person lies about the little things," he told her, "she'll lie about the bigger things, too. Not surprisingly, I later found out my fiancée had been withholding information about her past as well." Hunter involuntarily gritted his teeth at the memory of Yvonne's other secrets coming to light. "I ended the relationship and haven't regretted it a bit."

Julie swallowed and once again touched the paper in her pocket.

Strangely enough, he'd been having a disquieting feeling about Julie lately…as if she was withholding something, too. At first he'd thought she was being reserved, but that explanation didn't fit the robust young woman who had the habit of wearing her heart on her sleeve. *Reserved* was not a word anyone would use to describe Julie Beth.

Standing, she pulled the paper from her pocket and unfolded it. She looked as miserable as a jury foreman who was preparing to deliver a guilty verdict.

"There's something I need to tell you," she said just as the phone rang.

"Hold on a sec." He lifted a finger, then picked up the receiver. "Hunter Matthews."

He listened for a moment, narrowing his eyes as Julie watched. Abruptly, he interrupted his caller. "Are you calling from a secure phone?"

"Yeah," said the voice on the other end of the line. "I have some info that's going to shock you."

Hunter felt the blood leave his face as his informant finished delivering the unwelcome news. He clenched the phone cord with his free hand, which caused static to drown out the caller's voice. But that didn't matter. He'd heard all he needed to know. As he turned his body directly toward Julie, her pale blue eyes were enormous. The unfolded paper shook in her hand.

Julie waited while he finished his conversation, gathering her courage to confront him about the matter she had come in here to discuss. Though her job as a reporter was on the line, she found she no longer cared. He knew something, but how much, she hadn't a clue. It didn't matter. She wanted to tell him everything, explain why she'd done what she had. Let him know that she would accept whatever consequences came as a result of her concealment. And, most of all, find a way to make it up to him for deceiving him.

When he hung up the phone, he looked angrier than she'd ever seen him before.

"That was one of my moles," he said through clenched teeth. "It seems the new columnist at the paper is, indeed, someone who's close to me, but she's not my sister-in-law."

"I know." Julie twisted the paper in her hand, then attempted to smooth it out before handing it to him. "That's what I came in here to tell you."

"Oh, you did?" His brown eyes looked as black as the mood that had settled in the core of Julie's soul. "Was this another one of those 'pesky details' that you managed to lose track of?"

"It's not like that. A condition of getting the job permanently was that I keep it confidential."

She stepped closer, wanting to connect with him in some small way as she opened her heart about the matter she'd been trying to work up the nerve to tell him all along. But when he folded his arms across his chest, she knew this wasn't going to be as easy to set straight as a broken hand brake on a bicycle. Though she'd been terrified to go to him then and tell him about the mishap with his bike, and he'd been angry with her for riding it without his permission, he had still heard her out. She'd always been able to share everything with him—even the difficult things—and he'd always listened patiently.

But this time she'd gone too far. She hadn't just broken a possession, she'd broken his heart.

"Even so, I wanted to tell you anyway. It's just that the timing was never right."

"Uh-huh," he said. "I'm sure that's what Yvonne was thinking when she chose not to tell me about Len's phone call." His eyes were cold shards of obsidian as he hurled the words at her.

Julie understood his anger, but that didn't stop his reaction from hurting. He had planned to marry Yvonne, but he had cut her from his life for withholding information that she had believed to be inconsequential. Julie had not only withheld important information from him, but her failure to come forward right away had essentially made him look foolish. He'd never made any promises to her, so she had no hope—no expectation—that he would give her any more of a break than he'd given Yvonne. Not after Julie had lied knowingly and repeatedly about a matter that was crucial to him.

"Tell me, if you can," he said, "how your actions

are any different from what Anna or Yvonne have done?''

Julie drew her lips over her teeth and bit down to keep from crying. Unable to speak a word, either in her defense or in apology, she stood there mutely, shaking her head.

Her goal had been merely to get a job that would pay reasonably well and allow her to find her dream man at the same time. Considering the public's reaction to her test columns, she was probably a shoo-in for the position, but she no longer wanted it...not like this. And although she hadn't finished collecting the rest of her hundred kisses, she had, indeed, found her dream man.

But she couldn't have him. He was already wedded to integrity and honor, which left no room for someone like her. Someone who would—if not lie outright—lie by omission.

Sure, he fudged on the minor things when it came to catching dishonest people, but that was only so he could expose a bigger truth. Unfortunately, Julie had no bigger truth she was working toward. She had only a selfish desire to win a reporting job.

''I'm so sorry,'' she managed to say past the knot in her throat. ''I never meant to hurt you.''

Hunter walked to the office door and opened it. ''You need to get your things and leave,'' he told her coolly. ''We're finished doing business together.''

Julie opened her mouth, desperate to fill it with the words that would make things right again. But there were no such words. There was only regret for hurting—and now losing—the man she loved.

Chapter Nine

One of the strangest ironies behind the theory of kissing a hundred men before you marry is in the promise of finding a monogamous partner through polygamous smooching.

Hunter stood at the door of his office, frozen in place, as he watched Julie go to her desk and start gathering her belongings. When he was a teen, he had always marveled that someone so small could rile him so much. And now, a dozen years later, he was amazed that someone so beautiful and so sweet could hurt him so deeply.

Her hair, unencumbered by a clip, swung with her movements as she rearranged the piles of papers and folders on the desk. Having anticipated working in the office today, she had forgone her "spy-black" ensemble in favor of a bold pink sleeveless top and pale pink slacks. Her shoes remained uncharacteristically attached to her feet.

Something urged him to go to her. To take her in his arms and kiss away her obvious pain—pain that mirrored his own. But he could not. Recalling their previous kisses, he wondered if all of the subjects in her columns had believed, as he had, that their kisses were exclusive.

He'd never made a secret of the fact that he was a strong believer in playing by the rules. And those rules were what kept society from being swept along in a tide of chaos and disorder. They kept his office running smoothly and steadily. And the rules, when followed, were what kept people from stepping on each other's hearts.

His heart had been more than stepped on. It had been trounced, pummeled and flattened.

He should have made do without a secretary until Trudy returned. He was, after all, a one-secretary man. If he had just continued sharing Len's assistant, work would have piled up, but Hunter would have maintained a modicum of peace and order in the office. And in his soul.

The phone rang again, and Julie reached for it.

"Don't bother, I'll get it," he told her. "You just finish what you're doing."

When he came out a couple of minutes later, she was unplugging her radio.

"Congratulations, you've socked it to me again." When she looked up from what she was doing, a quizzical expression on her features, he said, "That was Trudy on the phone. She has decided to take your advice and quit her job."

Julie put a hand to her mouth, too stunned to know how to react. Given her previous track record with

Hunter, she doubted he'd believe anything she said, anyway.

He lifted his arm to look at his watch. "Two betrayals within five minutes. That must be a record for you."

"But I thought she—" Julie wanted to explain that she'd had no idea Trudy was planning to give notice. That she'd thought his secretary was thinking of starting a family. But she could only manage to stammer, "I—I merely suggested she follow her heart."

"Really?" He stepped over the threshold into what, until a few minutes ago, had been her work area. "Is that what you were doing when you were kissing men indiscriminately? Following your heart?"

Julie set the radio on the desk with a thump. "I've *never* kissed anyone indiscriminately," she insisted. Then, willing him to believe her, she added softly, "Especially not you."

He turned away, the gesture effectively telling her that his mind—and, most likely, his heart—were closed.

"Should I be expecting any more surprise phone calls, Julie?" he asked, turning back to face her once again. Even at his most tired, he was not the kind of man to lean against things, but now he rested one hand on the back of her guest chair, as if needing its support. "Is there anything else you need to tell me, but haven't?"

"Only that—" Only that she loved him. But there was no way he'd believe her if she said that, even though it was the truth. "Only that I've really enjoyed my time here, working with you."

He straightened and rested his hands on his hips.

Although he wore a smile, it was not the kind that bespoke humor or happiness or fond feelings. Rather, it was cynical and perhaps even a bit caustic.

"Which part did you enjoy?" he probed. "The part when you were working for the agency, or the part when you were collecting samples for your column?"

Devastated at having lost Hunter, Julie accepted that she'd get on with her life. She probably wouldn't get the job she wanted, but she'd find another. And she'd be happy.

Not as happy as if Hunter were in her life, but she'd do fine. That's what she kept telling herself.

She had been wrong to look outside herself for fulfillment. The satisfaction she'd received from writing a successful column and helping Hunter solve his cases had shown her she'd made a mistake in looking for a husband and family to give her the love and acceptance she craved. It had been there all along, inside herself, but she hadn't taken the time to find it.

She was most definitely complete. And very, very alone.

When she failed to respond right away, he answered for her. "I know. It must have been when you were helping me to find the mystery kisser. That must have given you quite a laugh," he said bitterly.

"I never set out to deceive you, Hunter." *Or to fall in love with you.*

He waved his arm and turned as if to go back into his office. But then he stopped and spun around to face her once again. "You know, I probably should keep you on as an investigator. You're really good at playacting. So good, in fact, that you fooled me into thinking I was the only one you were kissing.''

''You *were* the only one.'' Julie gripped her purse tightly to her chest until she heard what sounded like plastic cracking. Probably the compact in her makeup case. But even if the mirror was to break, her luck could get no worse than what it was now.

''I read your columns.''

''It's not what it seems. I wouldn't lie to you about that.''

''Maybe not, but you lied about other things.'' Hunter handed her the radio and then balanced the jar of toffees on top. ''Goodbye, Julie Beth.''

Holding her breath for fear of losing the last shred of her composure, Julie lifted her chin and walked from the building. When she got to her car in the parking deck, the first of a thousand tears began to flow.

Something nagged at the back of Julie's mind. Something forgotten. Possibly even important.

At first she thought it might be tomorrow's column that she had forgotten. But she had faxed it this morning, so that wasn't it. Most likely, that one would be her final column—her swan song. In the morning, as Richmonders were reading it with their first cup of coffee, the deejays would be announcing the winner who had found the mystery kisser. And, by doing so, they would prove to her editor that she was unable to remain undercover on a story.

But the loss of the column was small compared to what else she'd lost today. Julie gripped the steering wheel tighter and blinked back a fresh surge of tears. From the time she was small, Hunter had been there for her anytime she needed him. When she had fallen and scraped her chin after trying to belly-ride a swing, he'd been there with a wet compress and soothing words. When she had signed up to compete in her school's track events, he'd taught her how to break quickly from the starting line. And when she had been about to leave for her first school dance, he'd told her she was pretty, and insisted on having the first dance, right there in her living room.

And how had she repaid him? By putting a stupid column ahead of his feelings. At the time, that reporting job had seemed so important. But now...

Still, something felt undone. Considering the hasty manner in which she had left, it wouldn't be a surprise to discover she had forgotten something at the office. If that turned out to be the case, she would call Priscilla and ask her to meet her to deliver the items. There was no way she'd be able to go back to the office. Not now. Not after the way she had treated Hunter.

Reaching across the seat, she opened the flap on her purse and retrieved the day planner he had given her. Except for a scribble to calculate a restaurant tip and another notation recording a co-worker's birthday, the pages were empty. Now that she would be searching for a job to replace the reporter position she'd flubbed, it would soon be filled with interview appointments.

Perhaps Hunter was right. Perhaps she had gotten so caught up in whatever activity of the moment had captured her attention that she had lost sight of important details. Details that Gran had drummed into her head as a child, such as the "do unto others" admonition.

Well, she had done unto others, all right. There was Hunter, who had given her a job that she wasn't even qualified to perform, just because he was an honorable and decent sort of man. And she had repaid him by betraying his trust and leading him on a wild-goose chase. And then there was Anna Matthews who, though already doing a superb job of messing up her marriage, had received a helping hand from Julie and her column, making matters even worse.

If there was any way she could right the wrong she had done Hunter—no matter what the personal cost—she would do it. But she had already sealed her fate with him. That door was closed.

Perhaps, however, she could undo some of the damage she had inflicted upon his sister-in-law. It wasn't right that his relatives should suffer because of decisions Julie had made. If she'd been honest earlier, Hunter might have found out the truth behind Anna's surreptitious outings. And she and Peter could be working out their problems instead of divorcing over a misunderstanding—a misunderstanding that Julie had knowingly allowed to continue.

Taking a right onto Patterson Avenue, she drove to Anna's house and parked on the street in front of the neighbor's yard, where she attempted to formulate a plan of action. This was a time when it would be nice to have one of Hunter's scripted scenarios to guide her through what she was about to do. Something to keep her from overlooking any important details.

Anna's yellow Volvo sat in the driveway, testimony to her presence in the house. How, Julie wondered, did one go about approaching a relative

stranger and pointing out the error of her ways? And
how could she do so without coming across as the
hypocrite she was?

While she was deciding upon her course of action,
the stately front door opened and Anna stepped out
and squinted into the noonday sunshine. Slipping on
a pair of dark-framed sunglasses, the blonde walked
toward her car. Dressed in dark slacks and a royal-
blue top, with her permanent-waved hair falling casually around her face, Anna looked like an everyday
housewife setting out to run an errand to the grocery
store.

Apparently unaware of Julie's presence, she
backed her car out of the driveway and headed south,
in the direction of the mall. Remembering what
Hunter had taught her about remaining invisible
while following someone, Julie waited until Anna
was almost two blocks away before starting her own
car and pulling out onto the street.

Anna led her to a sports bar and turned into the
parking lot. A moment later, Julie followed her inside. It took a minute for her eyes to adjust to the
dim lighting, but sure enough, there at the end of the
bar was Anna, talking intently to a young man. A
very young man. With pimples.

This was worse than Julie had feared. Not only
was the almost-forty-year-old woman seeing another
man, she was also robbing the cradle. Julie drew a
fortifying breath and debated how and whether she'd
be able to convince her to leave her boy toy and
return to the husband who loved her.

"Smoking or non-smoking?"

"Neither," Julie said to the waitress who had ap-

peared at her side. "I see an empty place at the bar."
Right next to Hunter's sister-in-law.

So intent was Anna on talking to the fellow—the
boy—beside her that she failed to notice when Julie
slid onto the neighboring stool.

In a case like this, Hunter would probably tell her
not to call attention to herself. Just remain invisible.
Sit, listen and wait. But Julie's lack of forthrightness
had gotten her in trouble before, and she had no desire to repeat those disastrous results. So she chose,
instead, to take the direct approach.

Swiveling on the stool, she bumped elbows with
the woman beside her. "Hi," she said, holding out
her hand. When Anna turned to face her, and automatically responded, she added, "I'm Julie Fasano,
and I'd like to know why you would hurt your husband like this."

The startled woman attempted to withdraw her
hand, but Julie maintained a firm, meaningful grasp.

"Uh, I've gotta go now," said the red-faced youth
as he moved away from the bar.

Anna deliberately plucked her hand away from Ju-
lie's and thrust some bills at the panic-stricken guy.
Oh, good grief, was she paying him for his services?
This was even worse than Julie had thought.

When Anna turned back to her, she did so with a
directness that matched Julie's own. The woman's
hazel eyes seemed to penetrate her. "Do I know
you?"

"We haven't actually met before. But you may
have seen me a time or two in the past couple of
weeks."

"Your name is familiar," she persisted.

Julie felt a moment of unease. *She* was the one

who was supposed to be asking the questions. But considering her role in the deterioration of Anna's marriage, the least she could do was give her the information she sought.

"My family lived next door to your husband's family when I was growing up. I was a lot younger than Peter, but we used to see each other some when my sister Charlene and I visited Hunter."

"Oh, yes, I remember now," Anna said, her suspicious expression relaxing into a vague smile. "You were the barefoot little kid who used to follow Hunter everywhere. He couldn't turn around without bumping into you."

As if to reinforce what she'd said, Julie lost her grip on her dangling shoe, and it fell to the floor with a muffled thunk. She gave an embarrassed shrug.

Anna leaned forward and peered into her face. "Wait a minute. Are you the one who jumped into the fountain that night in Shockoe Slip?"

"Um, yes. That's what I wanted to talk to you about. You see, Hunter and I have been..." Julie fidgeted with her watchband, hoping she wasn't making things worse by having come here. "We've been sort of, um, following you."

Anna leaned back and crossed her arms over her chest. A hint of amusement danced at the edges of her mouth. With her pretty features, slim figure and obvious intelligence, she seemed to possess the necessary qualities for the wife of a judge. Too bad things were looking so bad in her marriage right now. But if Julie had anything to do with it, that matter would be fixed very shortly. If only she had a plan that could fix things with Hunter.

"You're kidding, right?" Anna reached over to

the bar and moved a thick manila envelope away from the puddle of condensation forming around her glass. "And was Hunter in the fountain with you?"

"Actually, that wasn't his fault. I sort of pushed him. Accidentally, of course."

Anna's response was not what Julie had expected. Having anticipated anger or guilt or denial, she was not prepared for the spurt of raucous laughter that burst from the demure-looking blonde.

"Oh, that's rich," she said. "What I wouldn't give to have a picture of Mr. Propriety landing butt-first in the water. I'll bet that wasn't on his minute-by-minute agenda, was it?"

Julie couldn't help responding to the woman's infectious humor. "In hindsight, I suppose it was pretty funny."

Like Anna, she would also treasure a photo of that moment, but for entirely different reasons. Unfortunately, a photo could never capture the warmth of his lips or the tantalizing strength of his arms as they wrapped around her body. Julie's photo—a bittersweet memory—would stay locked away in her heart.

Her mood now serious, she addressed the matter she had come here to confront Anna about. "That night at the fountain wasn't the only time we followed you," she said. "We know about your paramour."

Anna frowned, and her fingers tightened around the edges of the manila envelope. "My what?"

"Your boyfriend. You know," Julie said, jerking her head toward the chair her young lover had left vacant. "The guy you've been seeing these past few weeks."

"Him? He's the delivery boy."

"His socioeconomic status doesn't make what you're doing any more acceptable. Anna, you're breaking your husband's heart." She lowered her head, wishing to high heaven that Hunter hadn't been put in the position of telling the bad news to his brother. "Peter knows you've been sneaking around on him."

Anna stared at her the way a scientist might puzzle over an interesting new life-form. "Would you come with me to my house? We need to talk."

Stepping down from her bar stool, Anna gathered her things and waited for Julie to retrieve her shoe.

"While we're at it," she continued, hooking her free arm through Julie's and holding the envelope before her like a carrot, "I have something to show you."

The office outside Hunter's seemed emptier than ever before. Not just because the desk was tidier than it had been in the past three or four weeks. And not because the single men in the building found no reason to dawdle there after Julie had left. Rather, the room felt like a big, vacant space. Similar to the feeling that had settled deep inside him.

She'd only been gone a couple of hours at most, but the minutes had ticked by with excruciating slowness. When Julie had been here, time had adjusted itself to her presence, speeding up when he was trying to stay one step ahead of her unpredictability, and slowing to a near standstill whenever she was near enough for him to smell her perfume. When they had kissed, however, it became as erratic as the woman he had held in his arms, tick-tick-ticking like a time bomb, while he savored every sensual detail about her and committed it to memory.

Hunter shoved the grip-exerciser into his bottom drawer and rubbed the muscles in his hands and fore-arms. If he kept that up, he'd have carpal tunnel syndrome before the week was over. Telling himself he had no need for the gadget anyway, since the source of his stress was now gone, he rose and wandered into the other room.

Taking a seat and running a hand over the clean, polished surface of the secretary's desk, he marveled at the stark quiet that had returned to the outer office. No phone messages, flown toward his office in the form of paper airplanes, littered the carpet near his door. No stray shoes impeded the rollers on the swivel chair. And no radio broke the low, steady hum of the building's air-filtering system.

It should have felt peaceful. Or calm. Or orderly. But it felt like none of those things. Instead, the quiet loomed heavy and palpable.

Logic told him the strangeness that filled the room was merely due to the absence of a secretary to per-form the tasks that waited to be marked off the daily agenda. But those hours between Trudy and Mark's wedding and Julie's arrival hadn't seemed like this.

Hunter missed Julie, and since she had never been a good assistant, honesty prevented him from ration-alizing that he missed her as a secretary. As an in-vestigator, she'd always been able to "get her man," but even then, he'd never known what to expect from her. Despite her betrayals, both about her mystery-kisser identity and about her role in his secretary's quitting, he wanted to be near Julie.

The only explanation for his irrational response

was that he loved her. Hunter drew a deep, shaky
breath and raked his fingers through his hair. Sure,
he loved her beauty and her upbeat attitude and the
way she always looked a little bit dazed after they
kissed. But he also loved other things about her—
things that he'd once thought drove him crazy. The
way she turned a humdrum activity into play. And
the way he never knew what to expect when she was
around.

Hunter opened the shallow center drawer, thinking
maybe he'd find a nail file or a comb that would
make it seem as though she were here. But the pens,
paper clips and ruler were arranged as orderly as military soldiers. The sight should have comforted him,
but it only made him sad.

The side drawer was just as neat. It was as though
Julie had never been here. But when he opened the
bottom drawer, two items slid forward. One was a
lipstick tube. Hunter picked it up and twisted the base
to reveal the pinkish-red contents. The faint straw-
berry scent reminded him of the kisses they had
shared.

The other was a small, spiral-bound book. The
cover, embossed with miniature red lip prints, was
slightly dog-eared from age and handling. Curious,
Hunter set it on the desk and opened it. The pages
fell open to an early entry, a date that would have
had her a freshman in high school.

Name: Robert Wallace, senior and football captain.
Location: football field after a winning game.
Comments: Wally is much older than me and
way cool. (Cute, too!) After he scored the win-

ning touchdown, everyone rushed onto the field
and surrounded him. He high-fived the guys and
kissed all the girls, including me. It was really
sweet, even though it was only a cheek duster.
He saved the good one—a back-bender, one-
foot-in-the-air, hanging-from-his-neck kiss—for
his girlfriend, Kaye. Lucky girl.
Score: 4 3/4 for me, 9 for Kaye.

Flipping through the pages, Hunter noticed that
most of the entries, especially those written while she
was delivering singing telegrams, were about as innocent as the one she'd experienced with Wally.
Some of them seemed familiar, and when Hunter
read the journal passage about "Rank Frank" who
needed a breath mint, he realized she had drawn from
them for her newspaper column.

Curiosity overcoming caution, he flipped past the
college years and telegram recipients to the latest no-
tations. Entry number forty-seven belonged to
Hunter, "my childhood crush, but now with all the
added blessings that testosterone brings." A smiley
face graced the margin next to his name.

There was no forty-eight.

Hunter turned more pages to see if she might have
accidentally skipped a few, but the rest of the notebook remained blank except for the telephone numbers of two men, presumably the ones who had approached her at the tennis court. The hand-drawn
face next to these featured a little O instead of a
crescent for the mouth. A yawn.

As he slumped in the chair, the magnitude of what
he had discovered hit him between the eyes. Julie
hadn't kissed anyone after him. All those columns,

some of which he had pulled out and reread in an act of self-punishment after he had fired her, had been written about people she had kissed before him. People who ranked only a seven or lower in her book. Hunter's ratings, even for what he would have considered a "cheek duster," had tallied even higher than that.

Despite his earlier assumptions about Julie's veracity, Hunter was now convinced that, although she hadn't volunteered some important information about herself, she had, in fact, always been true to him.

She had not betrayed him. She had remained faithful, even when she'd had to resort to reporting on the low-scoring incidents in her book. Hunter's perception of the situation had been dangerously distorted.

Now, with this coming to light, he began to rethink his hasty reaction to her role in Trudy's quitting. If Julie had encouraged his secretary not to return to work, she must have had a good reason for doing so.

Pushing the desk drawer closed, Hunter stood and tucked the book in the pocket of his suit jacket. Just as he had been wrong about Julie, it was possible that he—and Peter—may have been wrong about Anna. With luck, his perception of her activities these past weeks had been as distorted as his notions about Julie.

With long strides intended to cover a lot of ground fast, he went down the hall to the elevator, calling out to the receptionist that he was going to his brother's house. Once there, he would try to convince Peter to try to work things out with Anna...just as he himself wanted to work things out with Julie.

Hunter prayed to God it wasn't too late.

Chapter Ten

Less than halfway to my goal, I've discovered that it isn't always necessary to collect the entire one hundred kisses. As our previous columnist, Ethel, once wrote, when the match is right, you just know. But what happens when you've found him and he doesn't want you?

In the driveway at Pete and Anna's house sat three cars, which was unusual for an afternoon in the middle of the week. His brother, something of a workaholic, rarely showed up before dinner, so the evidence that he had come home early stirred Hunter's anxiety.

More unnerving, however, was the fact that Julie was here, too. With a clammy uncertainty, he wondered what surprises lay in store for him now. Picking up his pace to jog across the groomed lawn, Hunter realized he didn't care, just as long as he saw

Julie again. And maybe even got a shot at trying to undo the mess he'd made earlier today. But he still couldn't help worrying that something was wrong for Julie to be here.

Though he rang the bell, he didn't wait for an answer, just opened the door and let himself in. Inside, Anna sat on the couch, looking dazed, with Peter beside her, his arm around her slender shoulders. Julie, having risen to come to the door, stood her ground, saying nothing.

"What's the matter?" Hunter demanded. "Are the boys okay?"

"They're fine. Julie sent them to the neighbors'," said Anna. "We've had a lot to discuss."

Hunter felt sucker-punched. Collapsing onto the couch, he remembered with sickening clarity the day someone had come to tell his mother that his father had been killed while on police duty. On that day, Hunter had been sent to the Fasano home, where Gran kept him occupied with chores until his mother was able to break the news to him.

Julie took a seat beside him, close enough that the gesture felt supportive, but far enough away to suggest she hadn't forgotten his unkind words today. Or maybe out of guilt, as if admitting that she had, yet again, managed to throw a kink in the works.

Whatever was going on, she definitely had something to do with it. It had to be something serious, he thought, for Peter to be holding his wife so intimately after having declared that he was going to insist upon a divorce. The two of them were giving each other looks that didn't fit the expected response in a case like this. And Hunter had seen more than his share of husbands and wives who had learned unpalatable secrets about each other.

"I'm sorry," Julie told the couple, "for butting into your personal matters. But I didn't know what else to do."

"There's no need to apologize," Anna assured her.

"We're grateful." Peter pulled his wife closer.

Anna smiled up at him and rested her head against his shoulder. "If I'd done things a little differently, or perhaps spoken up sooner, Julie wouldn't have been forced to step in and help unravel things for us."

Peter cleared his throat. "I was so wrapped up in work and concerned about what everyone else thinks that I might not have taken the hint. Sometimes it takes a brick upside the head to get my attention." He kissed his wife. "Hunter, you could take a lesson from me. Don't ever lose your sense of playfulness. Life is too short to go through it without humor...and a good woman."

When the two proceeded to whisper and snuggle like lovebirds, Hunter turned to Julie, hoping she could clear away the confusion. But she just shrugged, obviously pleased by the affectionate display between the couple.

Anna broke into his thoughts a moment later when she came up for air. "Hunter, why didn't you tell us the mystery kisser was working for you? You've been holding back." Then, with a playful dig of her elbow into her husband's side, she said to Julie, "I may call you to get some tips you learned during your research."

Hunter glanced toward Julie, who watched warily

for his reaction. Yes, she was definitely in the middle of whatever had just transpired between his brother and sister-in-law. And Hunter wanted to thank her for it, preferably with a kiss.

"Yeah, why didn't you tell us?" Peter prompted. "All along I was thinking Anna was the mystery kisser. Turns out my wife was working on a different mystery."

Hunter crossed an ankle over his knee. "It was a secret." From himself as well as everyone else.

Julie ducked her head and peered at him from beneath her lashes.

"Now that everything's coming out in the open," Hunter said, his attention fixed on Julie, "perhaps someone could fill me in on the latest developments?"

Out of the corner of his eye, he saw that his brother had other matters on his mind. Considering the way the couple was gazing at each other, he supposed this could take a long time.

Peter rose, cupping his wife's elbow. "Why don't you two go for a nice long walk?" he suggested, steering Anna toward the curved banister. "I'm sure Julie will be happy to bring you up to speed."

They disappeared up the stairs without another word.

Hunter stood and, hooking Julie's hand through the crook of his arm, nodded toward the front door. "It looks like they're going to be occupied for a while. A little exercise would probably do us some good."

Julie followed him outside, hoping the neighborhood sights would help erase the unlikely image of her and Hunter "exercising" together. Although he could only be pleased at the positive results she'd engineered, it was doubtful he would appreciate the manner in which she had gone about it. Not only had she broken protocol by contacting a subject and revealing what they had learned while following her, Julie wasn't even an employee of Oltmeier-Matthews anymore.

After they'd walked half a block, she removed her hand from his arm. "Today Peter saw his wife again for the first time in several years."

Hunter slowed his pace and sent her an uncomprehending look.

"Their eighteenth anniversary is coming up next week," she said, repeating the information that had been told to her. "Anna has been posing for romantic portraits, hoping the pictures—and a personal memoir of their early courtship—would help revive their marriage."

Although she herself had been thrilled to learn that Anna's intentions had been innocent, she feared that Hunter might react differently. They had all—Peter, Hunter and Julie—believed that Anna had been sneaking off for illicit meetings with a secret lover. And Hunter, chasing the possibility that Anna was also the mystery kisser, had been fooled twice.

"That bad essay," he said, "where he was denuding her foot…?"

"The first time she and Peter ever kissed."

Hunter gave a chuckle of the sort that a brother might use when he's just been handed some great ammunition against his older sibling. Then his tone turned serious. "What about when she was in the bedroom at that house where I was attacked by the dog? I know that wasn't Peter, because I had spoken to him just minutes before following Anna there.''

Julie skirted a tree root that had encroached on the sidewalk, and brushed arms with Hunter. He responded by slipping a guiding hand to the small of her back. At his touch, her skin tingled, but Julie refused to allow herself to enjoy it. They might be walking and talking together and demonstrating civility, but that didn't mean that anything could come from this moment of ceasefire. ''That was where Anna was having her boudoir photos taken. They're really very pretty, and quite tasteful. She let me take a look after she got them from the delivery boy.'' She paused, remembering another of the photos. ''There was even one of her in an elegant ballgown on the staircase of the Jefferson Hotel. Anna looked like a blond Scarlett O'Hara.''

Hunter studied her for a moment, and Julie felt the heat of his gaze.

''The photographer was her college roommate.'' The silence was disconcerting, and Julie felt compelled to fill it. ''She trusted her to be discreet.''

Hunter scowled. ''That doesn't explain why Anna was at a downtown business office the night you tried to climb the trellis.''

Julie smiled as she remembered what he had neglected to say. That was the night they had kissed in the fountain. A bittersweet longing filled her at the memory. ''Anna was going to take her out for dinner and drinks, but her photographer friend had to work late at the advertising agency, which was why she didn't stay very long.''

Hunter nodded and kept walking. After they crossed another street, he tucked his hands in his jacket pockets. An object filled the pocket on her side, and he gripped it tightly. "Pete said something about losing his sense of playfulness. Is that what the photos were supposed to do? Bring back the fun he and Anna used to have?"

A young girl was riding a bicycle toward them, teetering slowly as she tried to maintain her balance. Julie gave her a thumbs-up sign as she passed. "After Anna and I explained everything to each other, she called Peter and asked him to come home early. It took a lot of convincing, because he had to reschedule his docket, but after he came home he was glad he did." It was too bad it had taken him so long to give his marriage first priority, but the important thing was that he now understood how seriously a relationship could deteriorate when it was put on the back burner. "I think Peter realizes there's more to life than work, schedules and worrying about public opinion."

Hunter took her hand as they crossed a third street and stepped around a hopscotch game in progress. "I remember when they first met—how much fun they used to have. Always laughing and going places together. After the kids came, though, things seemed to change between them."

"That may have been part of it. There was probably a combination of factors. I'm just glad they decided to work things out before it was too late." Julie sighed, wishing it weren't too late for her and Hunter to make things right.

A large For Sale sign graced the lawn of the next house they passed. "Oh, how beautiful," she exclaimed.

The two-story, blue frame house with white shutters, if miniaturized, could have passed for a doll house. The gabled roof and broad front porch gave it a welcoming appearance, and the stone path up to the steps seemed to beckon them inside. Hunter, too, appeared captivated by its charm. The garage door was up, and Julie pictured him in there, changing the oil in a car or building a soapbox racer with his son. And his wife would step out the side door to announce that dinner was ready.

Julie's heart ached at the realization that the woman calling him to dinner would not be her. Peter had almost lost the woman he loved because he had made work his first priority. And Julie had indeed lost the man she loved because she had foolishly put the reporting job she wanted ahead of being honest with Hunter. And now she had neither.

Silently—and mercifully—Hunter continued on past the house, unaware of the torturous turn her thoughts had taken.

"Anna was always the one who took the initiative," he said, returning to their earlier train of conversation. "She was the one who thought up fun trips for them to take. And even day to day, she found fun in little things, like drawing silly faces on homemade cookies or playing word games at the dinner table. My brother, on the other hand, has a tendency to be too serious much of the time."

"A trait that runs in the family?" Julie cast him a teasing grin. She paused for a moment to take off her shoes. Holding them in one hand, she walked barefoot in the grass along the sidewalk.

Hunter's expression became more thoughtful as he considered her question. "Touché."

She touched his arm. "That was a joke."

He flashed her a brief smile and covered her hand with his. "All humor is built on at least a hint of truth. You're right, I'm more like my brother than I had realized."

At the next intersection, he turned left. They would circle the block and return to Pete and Anna's. While the couple was coming together to forge a stronger bond in their relationship, Julie and Hunter would soon be going their separate ways.

"When Peter became a judge, he grew even more serious than ever," Hunter continued. "It didn't seem unusual at the time, because he was working so hard to establish a reputation as a professional. But now, in hindsight, it's easy to see that he tried to rein in Anna, as well."

Hunter hadn't released his grip on her hand, and Julie leaned closer as they walked. He smelled good—clean and sporty. She remembered having seen his cologne in his desk drawer, lined up neatly beside a fresh shirt and tie that he kept for an emergency quick change. His whole life was like that. Neat. Orderly. Planned down to the smallest detail.

The exact opposite of her own.

"Your brother's a good man," she said in Peter's defense. "He wanted what was best for his family. He just happened to go a little off course with his good intentions."

"A *lot* off course, judging by how close they came to getting a divorce. Anna tried so hard to be the kind of person he was trying to mold her into, but it only hurt their marriage."

Hunter stopped and turned to face Julie squarely. His handsome face was creased by worry lines between his eyebrows.

"He was a fool," he stated.

When Julie tried to answer, he clutched her hand tighter.

"I was a fool, too," Hunter confessed. "I made the same mistake Pete did, trying to mold you to fit my own personal style instead of appreciating you for your unique qualities. Instead of appreciating that our differences are what make us complete."

Julie stood there, stunned, as he rubbed his thumb over her knuckles. She dared not allow herself to believe what she hoped he was saying.

Pulling her to him, Hunter wrapped his arm around her and continued their walk. He rubbed his eyes with the heel of his other hand, wondering why he hadn't seen this simple truth before. Why he hadn't recognized that, since his father's unfortunate death, he had become rigidly inflexible in his attempts to choreograph all aspects of life—his own and others'? Belatedly, he realized that he had been trying to "fix" everything on which Julie had left her mark of spontaneity. As if she were wrong and he were right, when in fact they just *were*.

All along he had thought that the problem was Julie's. But now he understood that his quest for perfection had been the biggest mistake.

For the first time in his life, he understood that everyone was entitled to make mistakes—even the man whose failure to follow safety precautions had caused his father to die. As for Julie, her mistake had been in withholding the truth from him. But his own blunder had been in trying to create absolute perfection, and squelching all spontaneity and fun in the process. The only way he could clear the slate was to forgive those mistakes, starting with his own.

By now, they had circled the block and returned to Pete and Anna's street. But they were still several blocks away, which left Hunter time enough to try to make things right. The rest, he knew, was up to Julie.

He didn't look at her—was unable to look at her—as he spoke what was in his heart. Even so, her beautiful face was imprinted in his mind's eye.

"Julie, I know I don't deserve it, but I was hoping you might find it in your heart to forgive me." She stopped where they were, forcing him to meet her gaze. Her pale blue eyes were full of kindness and hope. What he saw there encouraged him to continue with his confession. "I've been a big jerk, and you would have every right to hold it against me. Like Peter, I had the mistaken impression that my way was the best way. But now I know that we have to give each other space to be who we are. Even if the other person is not exactly like us." He lifted her hand and held it to his chest. "*Especially* if the other person is so different and so special that she fills my days with one surprise after another and keeps me from being an old fuddy-duddy."

She seemed stunned. This was one of the rare times when she did not have a ready reply for him.

"Hunter, I'm the one who needs to be forgiven," she said after a long, excruciating pause. "I had no right to deceive you the way I did. You were right to fire me, and I wouldn't blame you if you never wanted to speak to me again."

He shook his head, halting her words of protest. Having circled back toward Anna and Pete's, they returned to the blue frame house she had admired earlier. He motioned for her to sit on the low brick wall in front of it. When he joined her, he was aware of something in her eyes. A teary mist of remorse clung to her lashes, but there was something else. Confusion, perhaps?

"We both carried a good thing too far," he said. "I went too far in trying to achieve the impossibility of perfection. And you went too far in tricking the city's newspaper readers when you caught me in your web of deceit."

Her guilty response told him she misunderstood his intent. Since he was having trouble choosing the words that matched his feelings, he decided to show her instead that he wanted to put all this behind them.

Reaching into his jacket pocket, he retrieved the tiny notebook and handed it to her.

She put her shoes back on in a gesture that seemed to indicate she was preparing to bolt. Opening the book, she glanced at a few entries, her expression sad and full of regret. Then, shutting it again, she turned to him. "If you want to give my name to the radio station and collect the contest prize, I'll understand."

Hunter grasped her hand, twining her fingers with his. "What, and have every man in town wanting kisses from the woman I love?"

She looked down at the hand that covered hers. Large, strong fingers conveyed their owner's work ethic and determination to have whatever he set his mind on. Fingers that needed only be crooked to have her running to him.

She dared not wish for what could not be, but he had mentioned love. Was he opening a door for them to enter together? Or closing it gently, hoping to end things on a more positive note than the one they'd parted on this afternoon?

While she was wondering how to respond, Hunter abruptly switched topics. "Trudy has decided to open a home business, designing Web pages. She'll be her own boss," he added thoughtfully. "Guess I'll have to find a different way of getting the office work done."

Julie straightened and pulled away from his touch. He had answered the question that lingered in her mind. "Are you asking me to come back and work for you?"

It didn't seem logical, given his understandably negative reaction to her unwitting role in Trudy's quitting. But maybe Hunter was desperate. He would *have* to be to ask her to return to a job she had handled with only mediocre success.

He laughed. "No, of course not. You're not cut out for secretarial duties."

She might have taken umbrage at his words if he hadn't been so on target with his assessment. "I'm sorry you lost such a wonderful employee. If I'd had any idea she was thinking of—"

"No," he said, cutting her off. "Trudy's quitting was my own fault. As Peter said, sometimes it takes a brick to his head to get his attention, and the same holds true for me. Must be a Matthews trait," he added with a grin. "Anyway, you opened my eyes to the fact that I can sometimes go too far in my demands for perfection and order."

"You don't say." She didn't mean it the way it came out. Rather, she was stunned that, even if he did understand what she'd been trying to tell him all along, he would admit it out loud.

He acknowledged her impulsive comment with a conciliatory nod. "Because of my insistence on nothing less than one hundred percent perfection, I ultimately drove away the best secretary I ever had."

For a split second, Julie thought he was talking about her, but reason quickly returned as she realized he meant Trudy. Julie's shoulders drooped.

"Trudy didn't quit because of you," she countered. "She just wants to start her own business."

Hunter shook his head. "Maybe so, but I sensed some relief when she gave her notice."

Remembering the tight-lipped expression Trudy had given her when she had commented on their mutual perfectionism, Julie supposed that may have been true.

Pushing her hair away from her face, Hunter let his knuckles graze her jawline and the earring that dangled from her lobe. Then he rested his hand lightly on her shoulder. "I'll get over losing my secretary," he told her, "but I can't bear to think of losing you."

Now thoroughly confused, Julie lifted her face to the man who was playing havoc with her emotions. Crazily, she wondered if he might be talking to someone standing behind her. But his gentle smile and encouraging squeeze of her shoulder convinced her that she held his full attention.

He waited a long moment, as if expecting a response, but Julie could only wonder if this were a marvelous dream. She was unable to say a word for fear of breaking the spell that had settled over them. A bird warbled from a nearby tree, mirroring the song in her heart.

"Julie, this is rather sudden, but I want you to marry me."

Her mouth fell open. Hunter lifted his hand to her cheek.

"Yes, I know it's shocking, but so was the revelation I had after you left this afternoon. If you'll say yes," he said, rising to his feet and drawing her up with him, "I promise to be more spontaneous."

"Hunter, don't change for me." Julie threw her arms around his neck. "I love you just the way you are."

"That's a yes?" he said, gazing down at her.

"Yes, yes, a million times yes!"

He smiled, and Julie's soul filled with light.

"Here's one for the book, then." And he proceeded to kiss her in a way that might have seemed conspicuous in a neighborhood full of small children. It scored off the chart.

When he finally ended the kiss—much too soon, in Julie's opinion—he turned and tucked her under one arm. "I *have* to be more spontaneous," he said with emphasis. "A woman like you? Who kisses like that? It wouldn't be right to pair you up with an old fuddy-duddy for a husband."

He pointed toward the blue house that had caught her fancy. "And to show you just how spontaneous I can be, I think we should buy that house."

Julie gasped and pressed a hand to her heart. If he threw any more surprises at her, she might just collapse.

He lifted his shoulders and gave an unconcerned humph. "Or we could find a bigger one, if this doesn't suit. But I have to tell you, old habits die hard. The planner in me thinks this location is great, being so close to Pete and his family. When the time comes, Anna could baby-sit...or if she's busy, the boys will be old enough by then. I think we should have two."

Julie's voice squeaked. "Two baby-sitters?"

For the first time in her life, she understood why people often reacted with a dazed expression whenever she vocalized her skittering trail of thoughts. Hunter had thoroughly boggled her mind.

"No, two *kids*. One of each. Unless, of course," he said, gesturing toward her waistline, "you decide otherwise."

Through her adventures with Hunter, Julie had learned that kisses were only truly satisfying when they were shared between two people who loved each other. Seeing the look of complete acceptance in his eyes, she knew that his love was a joyful bonus to the friendship and respect that bound them.

Lifting her head, she invited him to kiss her once again, but this time it was a tentative, sweet touch, marking the beginning of a new life for them. And, to join him in that new beginning, Julie knew that she had to make a certain change of her own.

As they reluctantly pulled apart, she savored the taste of him on her mouth. They turned and began walking back toward Peter and Anna's house.

"If you're going to be more spontaneous, someone's going to have to pick up the slack in the area of handling details," she said, slanting a smile up at him and hooking her arm around his waist. "I promise to be more organized. Fortunately, I have the perfect day planner to help me do it."

"Good. You'll need it in your new job."

She tilted her head, considering the possibility.

"Let me guess. I did such a great job helping you solve your cases, you want me to come to work as a detective in your agency."

He had the nerve to laugh at that suggestion!

"After you left the office, I made a call to my source at the *Richmond Reporter*. He did some checking and found that you've been added to the newspaper's permanent payroll. Congratulations."

Julie halted in her tracks. "The columnist job is mine? But I thought, since I wasn't able to keep my identity a secret…"

"You stirred the interest of readers. Which increased newspaper sales. And which increased your editor's satisfaction with your column. He has to look at the bottom line, and you scored big in that regard."

"Oh, goodness, I'm so happy I could dance."

At that, Hunter swept her into his arms and twirled her twice, mindful of the book she still clutched.

"Now that I've turned over a new leaf," he told her, "I wouldn't dream of stepping on your spontaneity. But I have to admit that I'm rather selfish when it comes to sharing your kisses with other men."

Julie laughed. Now that he had turned over his new leaf, it seemed that nothing was holding him back. She looked forward to learning many more new facets of this man who would be sharing her life.

"The kissing series was just a test subject. Now is a good time to move on to something else," she assured him, and noted his pleasure at her words. "Most likely, I'll still be reporting on Gran's bits of wisdom, but in the future my columns will be based on personal interviews, not necessarily firsthand experience.''

Julie walked over to a garbage can that sat by the curb and lifted the lid to toss in her notebook.

Hunter stopped her with a hand around her wrist. ''Don't you want to keep that for a chuckle when you're eighty years old?'' he asked.

''You and your kisses are all I need.''

He tucked it back in his pocket anyway. And they kissed again.

Epilogue

There are many different kinds of kisses—warm and mushy, light and tingly, hot and passionate, and too many others to mention. But rather than sit here and write about them, I think I'll go practice them with the man I love. With any luck, it will take years to try them all.

Julie shifted her weight from one foot to the other. The first of the bridesmaids had already marched up the aisle, leaving Julie, her sister and their father waiting in the church entryway.

Clutching her nosegay to her lilac bridesmaid dress, Charlene bent and fussed with the hem of Julie's gown. "Stand still. You're turned up in front."

"I can't stand still. These shoes are killing me."

Charlene rolled her eyes in big-sister fashion. "I thought you would have outgrown that complaint by now. If you can plan a big wedding like this and keep track of all the deadlines and details, you should be able to keep your shoes on for more than five minutes.''

As her father gave Char a push to send her on her way, Julie snorted to hold back a laugh. Then she smiled with smug satisfaction at the compliment her sister had just given her. Determined to fulfill her promise to Hunter, Julie had seen to the gown and bridesmaid dresses, flowers, music, food and a zillion other items in the intricate planning process. It had been hard work, but with some organizing help from her day planner, and advice from the wedding planner and Hunter, everything had come together flawlessly.

And while she'd been busy with all that, Hunter had been actively working on being more spontaneous. Her heart warmed as she recalled a trip to the mall during which he had impulsively insisted they step into the photo booth for instant pictures. They'd had such a great time clowning around, and the joy had shone so brightly on their faces, that he'd suggested they use a particularly endearing pose on the front of their wedding invitation.

The organist glanced to the foyer, where Julie and her father waited, then lifted her hands dramatically and launched into the march music. Their cue had sounded.

Hunter already stood near the preacher, flanked by his brother. Peter surreptitiously patted his pants pocket, as if affirming the ring was still there.

Julie's gaze went back to her groom as she grasped her father's arm and began the slow procession up the aisle. Aware of nothing but the smiling man at the front of the church, she committed the sight to memory, determined never to forget how handsome he looked.

His dark, thick hair had been temporarily tamed with the judicious use of comb and water, and his eyes seemed almost to sparkle under the light of the chandelier. His lips curled upward with barely constrained merriment—a devilish expression that he wore quite often these days.

The tuxedo fit smoothly over his shoulders, accentuating their breadth, and continued in a clean line down his slim torso. The trousers lay snug against his muscled thighs and stopped just past his ankles.

Beneath the hems were a suntanned pair of large bare feet, toes curling in mischievous anticipation.

Startled at the unexpected sight, Julie stopped in her tracks, almost knocking her father off balance as she instinctively pulled against his arm. Her gaze flashed upward to Hunter's face, and his smile broadened so that it reached almost ear to ear.

The rascal! He clearly was taking very seriously his vow to be more spontaneous. Murmurs and giggles swept through the crowd of guests as they became aware of Hunter's unorthodox attire, but the challenging gaze that he fixed on Julie made it clear that he was unaware of everything and everyone but her.

Her father gave her a tug, reminding her that they still had half the length of the church left to walk.

Returning Hunter's grin, Julie kicked off her white pumps and joined him at the altar. She couldn't wait until tonight when they started their private investigation together...of each other.

* * * * *

SILHOUETTE *Romance*™

**Lost siblings, secret worlds,
tender seduction—live the fantasy in...**

A TALE OF THE SEA

**Separated and hidden since childhood,
Phoebe, Kai, Saegar and Thalassa
must reunite in order to safeguard
their underwater kingdom.
But who will protect *them*...?**

July 2002
MORE THAN MEETS THE EYE
by Carla Cassidy (SR #1602)

August 2002
IN DEEP WATERS
by Melissa McClone (SR #1608)

September 2002
CAUGHT BY SURPRISE
by Sandra Paul (SR #1614)

October 2002
FOR THE TAKING
by Lilian Darcy (SR #1620)

*Look for these titles wherever
Silhouette books are sold!*

Silhouette®
Where love comes alive™

SRTOS

If you enjoyed what you just read,
then we've got an offer you can't resist!

Take 2 bestselling
love stories FREE!

Plus get a FREE surprise gift!

Clip this page and mail it to Silhouette Reader Service™

IN U.S.A.	IN CANADA
3010 Walden Ave.	P.O. Box 609
P.O. Box 1867	Fort Erie, Ontario
Buffalo, N.Y. 14240-1867	L2A 5X3

YES! Please send me 2 free Silhouette Romance® novels and my free surprise gift. After receiving them, if I don't wish to receive anymore, I can return the shipping statement marked cancel. If I don't cancel, I will receive 6 brand-new novels every month, before they're available in stores! In the U.S.A., bill me at the bargain price of $3.34 plus 25¢ shipping and handling per book and applicable sales tax, if any*. In Canada, bill me at the bargain price of $3.80 plus 25¢ shipping and handling per book and applicable taxes**. That's the complete price and a savings of at least 10% off the cover prices—what a great deal! I understand that accepting the 2 free books and gift places me under no obligation ever to buy any books. I can always return a shipment and cancel at any time. Even if I never buy another book from Silhouette, the 2 free books and gift are mine to keep forever.

215 SDN DNUM
315 SDN DNUN

Name	(PLEASE PRINT)	
Address	Apt.#	
City	State/Prov.	Zip/Postal Code

* Terms and prices subject to change without notice. Sales tax applicable in N.Y.
** Canadian residents will be charged applicable provincial taxes and GST.
All orders subject to approval. Offer limited to one per household and not valid to current Silhouette Romance® subscribers.
® are registered trademarks of Harlequin Books S.A., used under license.

SROM02 ©1998 Harlequin Enterprises Limited

**Where royalty and romance
go hand in hand...**

The series continues in Silhouette Romance
with these unforgettable novels:

HER ROYAL HUSBAND
by Cara Colter
on sale July 2002 (SR #1600)

THE PRINCESS HAS AMNESIA!
by Patricia Thayer
on sale August 2002 (SR #1606)

SEARCHING FOR HER PRINCE
by Karen Rose Smith
on sale September 2002 (SR #1612)

And look for more Crown and Glory stories in
SILHOUETTE DESIRE starting in October 2002!

Available at your favorite retail outlet.

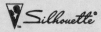

A powerful earthquake ravages Southern California...

Thousands are trapped beneath the rubble...

The men and women of Morgan Trayhern's team face their most heroic mission yet...

A brand-new series from *USA TODAY* bestselling author

LINDSAY McKENNA

Don't miss these breathtaking stories of the triumph of love!

Look for one title per month from each Silhouette series:

August: THE HEART BENEATH
(Silhouette Special Edition #1486)

September: RIDE THE THUNDER
(Silhouette Desire #1459)

October: THE WILL TO LOVE
(Silhouette Romance #1618)

November: PROTECTING HIS OWN
(Silhouette Intimate Moments #1185)

Available at your favorite retail outlet

Where love comes alive™

COMING NEXT MONTH

#1612 SEARCHING FOR HER PRINCE—Karen Rose Smith
Crown and Glory
Sent to Chicago to find a missing prince, Lady Amira Sierra Corbin
found—and fell for—a gorgeous tycoon. Skeptical of Amira's
motives, Marcus Cordello hid his true identity. Would love conquer
deceit when Amira finally learned the truth?

#1613 THE RAVEN'S ASSIGNMENT—Kasey Michaels
The Coltons: Comanche Blood
Was the presidential candidate leaking secrets that could threaten
national security? Agent Jesse Colton intended to find out—even if it
meant posing as campaign staffer Samantha Cosgrove's boyfriend!
But would this unlikely duo find the culprit...and discover love?

#1614 CAUGHT BY SURPRISE—Sandra Paul
A Tale of the Sea
Beth Livingston's father was convinced that mer creatures existed—
and now had living proof! But was the handsome merman Saegar
willing to become human in order to protect his underwater kingdom
and escape captivity? And what would become of Beth—his new
wife?

#1615 9 OUT OF 10 WOMEN CAN'T BE WRONG—Cara Colter
When Ty Jordan's sister entered him in a contest, 90 percent
of the women declared Ty the most irresistible man in the world!
Ty, however, wasn't interested in their dreams. Could photographer
Harriet Snow convince Ty to make her the object of *his* fantasies?

#1616 MARRIED TO A MARINE—Cathie Linz
Men of Honor
Justice Wilder had led a charmed life—until an injury forced
him to rely on his ex-wife's younger sister. As a physical therapist,
Kelly Hart knew she could help heal his body, but could she
convince Justice that she wasn't another heartless Hart?

#1617 LIFE WITH RILEY—Laurey Bright
Handsome, successful Benedict Falkner wanted the perfect society
wife—*not* someone like Riley Morrissette, his beautiful, free-spirited
housekeeper. Still, the thought of having Riley in his life—in his
bed!—was nearly irresistible....